AN ARRANGED MARRIAGE

It's 1820 in South Yorkshire, and Patricia Pickering is wealthy, but lonely. A young widow and inheritor of the Pickering Mill, she is also joint owner of the Flint mill with her cousin, Robert. Meanwhile, Lord Percy Alexander of Wakefield Hall, is responsible for its debts and the welfare of his two younger siblings. Though Robert has proposed marriage to Patricia, to benefit the running of both the mills, she finds that it's Lord Percy who's on her mind — after he'd nearly knocked her over!

BETH JAMES

AN ARRANGED MARRIAGE

Complete and Unabridged

LINFORD
Leicester

First published in Great Britain in 2011

First Linford Edition
published 2013

British Library CIP Data

James, Beth.
  An arranged marriage. - -
  (Linford romance library)
  1. Love stories.
  2. Large type books.
  I. Title II. Series
  823.9'2–dc23

  ISBN 978–1–4448–1503–0

Published by
F. A. Thorpe (Publishing)
Anstey, Leicestershire

Set by Words & Graphics Ltd.
Anstey, Leicestershire
Printed and bound in Great Britain by
T. J. International Ltd., Padstow, Cornwall

This book is printed on acid-free paper

1

'Robert, I am sorry. I thought I had made myself clear. It makes no difference however many times you ask me, my answer must always be the same. I do not wish to marry you.'

Patricia met the mulish look of obstinacy on the face of the young man sitting in front of her and allowed herself the vestige of a smile.

'We wouldn't suit. If you only allow yourself to think about it, you would own the truth of it.' The smile broadened into a grin which lit up her neat but unremarkable features into a quite compelling whole. 'You should look for a demure bride. A girl perhaps scarcely out of the school room; someone of placid disposition whom you can mould to your ways. Now, Robert, admit it — that girl is not me.'

No, she thought emphatically to

herself. *That girl is most definitely not me.* Patricia was a woman of six and twenty, a woman of business and a wealthy widow to boot; why on earth would she give up her newly-found independence to marry her cousin, merely for the sake of his convenience?

It was Papa's fault; of course it was. Fancy him leaving the Flint wool mill in the equal care of his daughter and his brother's son. What a nonsensical notion! Although she recognised a second later that, at the time her father had made his will, there was no way of knowing that shortly after his own demise, his son-in-law would also take to his deathbed. He had probably surmised that with Patricia owning half the Flint mill, Robert would allow himself to be guided at least in part by Felix, who was after all an experienced mill owner himself.

Patricia pursed her lips. The fact still remained, however, that her husband had outlived her father by a mere six months and consequently, she was now in what some would opine was the enviable position of owning one and a half mills.

It was Patricia who had helped to transform her late husband Felix Pickering's woollen mill from an inefficient, run-down money pit to a small but modern and well-functioning mill, complete with contented workers — no mean feat, she acknowledged to herself with pride. But now Felix was dead and, on her solicitor's advice, she was in the process of negotiating its sale to the owner of the mill sited next door to Pickering's on the river Calder.

It made sense to sell it. The two mills could easily be integrated and prove even more successful, benefiting the area in general and the large family, predominantly made up of young male members, who ran the neighbouring enterprise in particular.

The Flint wool mill was a different thing altogether.

'The mill is still doing well, I trust, Robert?' she inquired.

With no change in his sulky expression, Robert Flint shifted in his chair. 'Aye, it's doing well, but the knowledge that it only belongs in half to me does, I think, weigh with the workers. They've never worked for me in the way they did for your father . . . But knowing that half has been left to you — a woman . . . ' He paused and put a hand to his neck-cloth, the bloodstone ring on his finger sparkling as he re-arranged its snowy folds. 'That's why — surely you can see — it would be a most desirous thing if you married me and we could keep our business in the family?'

And that is most precisely why I will never consider the idea, Patricia thought to herself. She took a last sip of her tea and wondered how soon she could decently bring this interview to a close. Aloud, she continued, 'Robert, I think I have earned a rest. Being my father's only child, I helped first Papa, then Felix with the running of their businesses. I also nursed Papa through his last illness. Then Felix dying so suddenly . . . '

She looked away and bit her lip. After a pause she went on, 'You know my plans for the Pickering mill. The proceeds I recover from the sale will be large, and will mean that I can do many things I've only ever dreamed of. The half share I hold in Flint's woollen mill need not cramp your style. I take no salary and leave the running of the mill in the main to you . . . No, you have a good mill manager, good workers — and you yourself could easily become proficient in all aspects of the business.

'If at some time in the future you come to consider buying my share, I shall be only too happy to discuss terms — of course, in the presence of Papa's solicitor John Standish.' She raised an enquiring eyebrow. 'Now if that's all — I have things to do.'

An angry flush stained Robert's cheeks as he got to his feet. 'You know perfectly well that your father meant us to marry,' he said petulantly. 'We are of an age, and that was why he left the mill between us — why else would he have done that?'

Patricia sighed. Any thoughts of her marrying Robert had been killed in her teenage years when she'd told her father quite frankly that the idea was abhorrent to her. But she knew exactly why Papa had written his will in such a way. He felt duty-bound to leave Robert something, but was anxious about his nephew's ability to make the correct decisions concerning the mill.

He had thought his daughter was secure in her marriage to the wealthy mill owner Felix Pickering, and did not dream that she would be made a widow at such a young age. But if Papa's ghost could only speak to her now, she was sure he would never recommend her to marry her cousin, because then Robert would gain total control over both the mill and Patricia — for good or evil. And while Patricia thought it would probably not be for evil precisely, she had a strong feeling it wouldn't be for good either.

She disliked Robert. She always had done, even when they were children. He was a year her senior, spoilt, and rather a bully. It was no good, she didn't like him, and didn't trust him and as for marrying him — well! Never.

Regarding him now, his hands clenched into fists at his sides and his usually quite handsome face set in a scowl, Patricia rose from her chair and tugged on the bell pull.

'What you say is absurd. Papa had no reason to think that Felix would die in his thirties — and even if he had, he never contemplated you and I marrying — you may be sure of that.'

'But . . . ' her cousin blustered.

'The conversation is over, Robert!' she said dismissively, not even bothering to smile this time.

Every inch the wronged hero, Robert regarded her with narrowed eyes.

'Don't think I've accepted this situation, Patricia. As the only male heir, the mill is my right and I'll find a way to make it so. You see if I don't!'

'Don't be foolish, Robert,' answered Patricia with a yawn. Then, turning as the butler came noiselessly into the room, 'Mr Flint is leaving now. See him out, please, Brooke. Oh, and I shall be dining in tonight — alone.'

But once Robert had left, Patricia abandoned all pretence of composure. She sat down rather suddenly, her mind in a whirl.

While it was true that in the last months she had succeeded in presenting a consistently calm, strong front to her friends and what was left of her family, on the inside she had been far from tranquil and utterly undecided as far as her future was concerned.

After the first shock of the sudden death of her comparatively young husband, she had clung tightly to the idea that she must continue to run the Pickering mill at all costs: that she would now deal with the farmers and wool merchants, the factories that produced the new carding machines for the production of their cloth. Then reality crept up on her.

In business terms, Felix and Patricia had been good partners. Felix had been a charming and persuasive tradesman. He was good at buying, better at selling and enjoyed all dealings of a social nature. Few of his industrial contacts, however, had any idea of the degree of influence Patricia wielded behind the scenes, improving inefficient practices and keeping the business running smoothly.

Suddenly she'd had to consider whether she would be an adequate substitute for Felix, who had always been so good-tempered, so amiable and so persuasive — in his gentle way — in bending people to his will.

She was, after all — as Robert frequently pointed out — only a woman.

And she felt mutinously that she *did* deserve a rest. Well, not so much a rest as, maybe, a different way of life.

Her marriage to Felix had been, if not exactly a mistake on a personal

level, then a disappointment. As Felix
had been in the same business as her
father, also based in the vicinity of
Wakefield, they had known each other
for some time. She had been immediately attracted to his good looks and
easy manner; he put her in mind of how
she'd always imagined a brother might
be. He had been a good companion;
they had liked one another, and the
marriage made good business sense.

Many times Patricia had told herself
that she was foolish to want more, for
Felix had never been less than kind and
companionable, but his visits to her
bedchamber had been rare and she'd
felt somehow incomplete and disap-
pointed when he left.

And she had never conceived.

Somehow after he'd died, it mattered
more. There seemed to be no one now
for her to care for, to work for or to
plan the future with. For a while
Patricia felt quite desolate.

The lawyer, John Standish, had
helped her to settle her affairs but

advised her that the matter of the Pickering mill could not wait indefinitely. Patricia knew this to be true; there was nothing worse for the workers than the prospect of an uncertain future so, suddenly wanting to be free of the responsibility, she agreed to sell.

It was only now, standing alone in the beautifully furnished reception room of the elegant three-storey Georgian house that Felix had bought for them to share, that she wondered what on earth she would do with the rest of her life. The house was large, yet comfortable, and situated in the best part of prosperous Wakefield — the centre of the clothing trade. But did she, in her heart, wish to remain here?

Suddenly restless, Patricia set off to tour the house. She started at the top, just below the servants' quarters. Opening and closing the upstairs rooms, her thoughts drifted to the unborn children — handsome and dark-haired like herself and Felix — whom she had thought would occupy them. She glanced into the best reception room, with its silk-covered chaise longue, Adams fireplace and Regency-striped window hangings. Slowly she made her way down the stairs again, pausing on the halfway landing to gaze through the deep, rectangular window at a world that seemed bleak indeed. As she stood looking out over the gravelled drive to the Yorkshire hills in the distance, she pulled her shawl snugly round her shoulders, then clasped her arms more closely still about herself in a child-like hug.

Oh, for a child — a baby to love and worry over. A new life — a whole new world to watch unfolding.

Sadly, she continued on her way down the stairs.

*　　★　　★*

It was past midnight. In the estate office of Wakefield Hall, the candles were guttering low in their ornate holders. Young Lord Percy Alexander pushed a lock of dark blond hair from his forehead, his usually lively, twinkling eyes serious for once.

'Only one thing for it, Fairbrass. An advantageous marriage — nought else to be done!'

The estate manager regarded him gravely from across what seemed to be wave after wave of parchment which flowed across the old oak desk between them.

'It would certainly seem so, my lord. In the short term we are able to pay off the more pressing debts — sell some of the horses, perhaps; reduce expenses somewhat — but in order to put the estate to rights we need a lump sum, and quickly.'

Percy gave a sigh. 'Should have realised what straits we were in . . . '

Fairbrass, who at five and thirty years was a decade ahead of his young master, looked at Percy with a certain amount of sympathy in his eyes.

'His late lordship would never hear of your being informed of the full picture, my lord. 'He'll know soon enough,' he used to say. 'Cut the lad some slack — he should enjoy himself whilst he may.''

For a moment the grim line of Percy's mouth relaxed and his lips twitched at the memory of his always smiling and genial father.

'No need to be mealy-mouthed about it, Fairbrass, Papa was no realist — was he?' He picked up the nearest paper to hand and pulled a wry face. 'Neither was he a mathematician, it would seem. You know of his extravagances as well as I do. Always spoke as though money was of no importance, as though something would give a turn to our fortunes . . . '

He threw the paper down and brushed an impatient hand across his brow again. 'I've just returned from the Grand Tour, for pity's sake . . . What was he thinking of, letting me go? Gave me to understand that the expense was no object, y'know . . . Should've made it my business to know more of our circumstances. Why didn't I see it?'

He lifted an arm and a wave of the paper before him fell to the floor.

'Oh well,' he murmured, more philosophically this time. 'Won't be the first son of a lord having to marry for money. It's come earlier than I have a taste for, but daresay I can make a decent enough job of it. Let's see now, the season is not yet upon us and we still have the London house — shabby as it may be. Although,' he raised his eyebrows enquiringly, 'perhaps it would be wiser to sell it?'

Fairbrass looked directly at him. 'Appearance is all,' he said ominously. 'If we sell the London house it will quickly be known that your pockets are to let, the banks might call in their loans and that would be nothing short of disastrous. Better to keep up appearances, use the town house — and find a rich bride — with all speed.'

'So — a season in London, then. Celebrations, balls, routs and assemblies. Riding in the park; attending the races and the soirees. Costly but necessary extravagance, eh? In my effort to catch a wealthy bride?' He turned away, a shadow of distaste in his eyes. 'Not that I object to London society to that degree — hope I enjoy a party as much as the next man — but can't say I relish the thought of the pretence and the subterfuge.'

There was a discreet cough. 'You know full well there will be many worse propositions than yourself on the marriage mart this season, my lord. You come from good family with a distinguished history. You are, after all, a lord. Your disposition — you'll pardon my commenting — I have always found to be pleasant. You own an extensive estate and your looks and bearing pass muster, if you will allow me to say so.'

Percy tried to resist the sudden tug of a smile but gave up as a chuckle escaped him. 'You are priceless, Fairbrass. I note you have not let the words 'fortune hunter' pass your lips, but that's what I shall undoubtedly be however you parcel it — and that, Fairbrass, is not a thought that brings me any pleasure at all.'

'Of course not, sir, but . . . '

Percy looked round sharply. 'But?'

'It has crossed my mind that perhaps the most expedient course of action in the circumstances,' went on Fairbrass, a note of cautious optimism creeping into his voice, 'would be for you to find an heiress locally. To allow London society to believe you have made a love match here in Yorkshire . . . '

A sardonic laugh escaped Percy's lips. 'Love match? Fail to see how that may come about — even if there is such a thing — which I doubt.'

Fairbrass shook his head. 'So young, yet so cynical,' he murmured.

'Well, my man, where do you suggest I am going to find an heiress in South Yorkshire? I've socialised with all the acceptable families of high standing in the area, and the daughters of marriageable age are colourless, simpering misses. Wouldn't want to share a bowl of porridge with them, let alone a marriage bed.'

'It was merely a suggestion, sir,' said Fairbrass in an injured tone. 'And, with apologies, my lord, might I point out that it is not only the members of the ton that hold the purse strings these days. We're prosperous here in South Yorkshire, especially in the Halifax and Leeds areas. The wool trade has done exceptionally well in recent years . . . You'd do well to think on it.'

In one fluid movement Percy rose to his feet. 'I know that what you're suggesting, Fairbrass, isn't entirely stupid, you know. An alliance with 'the trade'.' Percy gave a small shudder. 'But I do not think so, my friend. There are other ways to mend my fortune — bound to be.'

Fairbrass watched through calculating but not unsympathetic eyes as Percy stretched his arms above his head, unknowingly displaying his well-toned, taut body to its best advantage.

'If you should change your mind, my lord, I can make it my business to enquire as to the existence of any ladies of considerable means looking to find a place in the aristocracy.'

'What?' Percy was rubbing his eyes and barely listening now. 'You're a good fellow, Fairbrass, but I doubt the necessity.'

'There's Master John's education, of course, and it will soon be time for Katherine's coming out . . . Think on it. Goodnight, sir.'

Percy stopped rubbing his eyes and turned them back to the tide of parchment flowing over the desk to the floor. He balled his fist and smashed it towards the midst of the paper, just stopping short as he reached it.

He watched his estate manager's back as he left the room.

'I shall contrive,' he murmured in a quiet but firm voice. 'Somehow, I shall contrive.'

2

Percy looked up with some relief from the bill for payment he was holding as his estate manager knocked on the office door, saying, 'I have good news, my lord.'

'Then I'm entirely at your service, Fairbrass. Be the first good news I've come across for nigh on a week. Make yourself comfortable.'

Fairbrass looked around and pulled an old carver chair to the other side of the desk. Percy recognised for a fraction of a second that in fact this desk was the province of the estate manager and that he had seldom, if ever, seen the late Lord Alexander seated in the chair he had taken a habit of commandeering for himself in recent times.

He shifted in his seat and glanced at the man's weathered, ruddy face for any sign of resentment that he was encroaching on his territory. But Fairbrass sat down comfortably enough in the spare chair, crossed his legs one over the other and leaned forward.

'Do you remember that odd-shaped piece of ground — about two acres — at the north perimeter of the meadow land?'

Percy shook his head. 'Should I?'

'Not necessarily. It's of little importance — at the moment!'

Percy raised his eyebrows.

'I've heard a rumour — and it's only a rumour, mind — that the railway might be extending.'

'Railway eh? The one at Middleton Colliery?'

'That's the one.' The excitement showed in Fairbrass's eyes.

'You mean — ' rejoined Percy, looking interested now. 'You imply it might be possible that the railway company put in a bid for the land? But surely two acres can't be worth much, Fairbrass?'

'Well, if the alternative is to blast and

lay track through the outcrop of rock that's situated to the west of it, who knows? The rocky terrain is the reason the land is so awkward to utilise as anything other than grazing. Despite how level it is, it's nigh on inaccessible.'

Percy narrowed his eyes. 'So, what do you advise? Should we approach the railway company?'

'It wouldn't do to appear too eager and approach them direct. No, but it wouldn't go amiss to visit Standish, the solicitor your father used for matters such as this. Just in order to test the waters and to discover what the land may be worth . . . A casual enquiry. I needn't remind you that, at the moment, any extra revenue would be helpful.'

Glancing back at the demand for payment in his hand, Percy sighed. 'Certainly don't need reminding of that. Just finished making arrangements for half Papa's stable to go up for bid at Tattershalls, and that won't be the finish of it either. Most of the carriages will have to go . . . So as not to cause a stir, I'll put it about I consider them to be outmoded. Heaven knows, some of them are. The barouche, for example . . . ' He gave a shudder. 'Believe it belonged to my grandmother. And we surely don't need two open chaises with hardly a difference between them. And d'you realise, Fairbrass, what an extortionate amount we spend on candles?'

'Household accounts, my lord? I beg you will discuss those matters with Mrs Rivers.'

Percy blanched and dropped the bill as though it burned his hand. 'Oh well, dare say the candles will wait. I can't contrive to be quite comfortable with Mrs Rivers. Known her too long, and too many transgressions from the past come back to haunt me whenever I've to address her on even the most commonplace of matters . . . Should definitely make enquiries regarding this odd piece of land you speak of, though. We'll go examine it now, eh?'

With a pleased expression on his

face, Fairbrass rose to his feet.

'I thought you would agree, sir, and might I suggest, if the outcome should be favourable, that we waste no time in securing an early appointment with Standish.'

Halfway to the door he turned and eyed Percy speculatively. 'I could go alone, my lord, if you should prefer?'

'Not at all, Fairbrass. Intend to stay involved and take estate matters seriously. Know I've a lot to learn. I'll come with you — never fear. Don't want us to appear too anxious about the monies involved, though — eh? Perhaps best to convey to Standish that seeking experience is the reason I'm accompanying you, and that the novelty will soon wear off and I'll be back at the gaming tables in a trice. Know what I mean — young, green lord, somewhat wet about the ears seeks to improve knowledge of estate, that kind of thing — eh?'

'The notion had already occurred, sir,' answered Fairbrass, his expression deadpan.

* ★ *

Patricia leaned forward, her colour a little high. 'So, Mr Standish, I beg of you, please do not encourage my cousin Robert in his imaginings that I will in any way change my mind — for I won't — I shall never marry him!'

John Standish, a man of some twenty years' experience in dealing with his clients' wishes, regarded her over his steepled fingers and said nothing.

Wondering why it was that she seemed to feel so very angry this morning, Patricia shifted in her seat. 'Furthermore I should like you to refute any wild rumours that are circulating regarding my future. My future is just that — mine — to do with as I please. Shortly I shall let it be known via an official announcement that Pickering mill is to be under the new ownership of the Tate family.' She compressed her lips for a moment, trying to stem the fresh heat of sudden fury that overtook her, then went on in a tone that was more level, 'Robert was disillusioned enough to think that I would fall into his arms with gratitude, making him a present of the Pickering mill and the half share I hold in the Flint mill in the process. Never was he more wrong; Papa would turn in his grave were I to do such a thing.'

She swallowed a lump in her throat and blinked rapidly in an attempt to hide the distress that was still barely below the surface. That Robert could behave in such an oafish manner was beyond bearing: if only her father had been alive, he would have sent him about his business.

A fresh wave of sadness swept over her. She bit her lip. Of course she missed Papa; of course she still felt lonely.

There was the restrained sound of her solicitor clearing his throat.

Immediately she forced her lips to a smile. 'I'm sorry. I embarrass you.'

'No, my dear. I think you are making a prudent decision: it could only cause bad feeling between you and your cousin, were you to continue in your ownership of the Pickering mill. You are right to sell it, and have made a sensible choice as to the buyer. Should Mr Robert Flint ever find himself in a position to make an offer for your share in the Flint mill, I will certainly advise him so to do and I am quite sure that we can come to an arrangement that is good and proper.'

As she looked across the desk at the understanding countenance of one of her father's most trusted friends, Patricia regained her calm.

'Thank you,' she said quietly. 'I knew I could rely on you.'

'But what are your plans for the future, my dear?'

Patricia looked surprised. 'My plans?'

'Forgive me . . . From the way you spoke earlier, I thought you had something definite in mind.'

She shrugged. 'I'd thought perhaps of travel. I have always wanted to see Italy and France, and now that the war is a thing of the past . . . But, well,

27

somehow the idea is not so attractive when one is alone.'

Thoughtfully John Standish regarded her, before smiling benignly.

'Well, you are already comfortable. The house in Wakefield is bought and paid for, the proceeds from the sale of Pickering's and the steady income from your shares in the Flint mill, not to mention the shares in the railway that your maternal grandfather left you . . . '

'Ah yes, the advantages of being an only child.' Patricia bent her head in thought. 'The disadvantage, of course, is the loneliness.'

Then she collected herself, looked up once more and met the kindness in her solicitor's eyes with a sudden, wide smile. 'But I mustn't dwell on that. Being sorry for myself is the last thing I should be, in the circumstances.'

'Come now, it's only natural that you should miss your father — you were very close and it's not so very long since his death.'

She nodded. 'Yes, but it hardly seems so.'

'And then the sudden death of your husband.'

'Yes, that shock was painful also.'

'Perhaps your cousin was a little presumptuous, a little insensitive to push his suit so speedily.'

Patricia gave a restrained smile. 'If he had only taken time to consider, he would have known we should not suit each other.'

John Standish placed his hands flat against his desk. 'I can see you are adamant on that score. But you're a young woman with all of life before her. You're surely not dismissing all ideas of a second marriage?'

This time a half-laugh of amusement did escape her. 'If I didn't know you to be a family man yourself, Mr Standish, I would have almost taken that to be a proposition.'

The solicitor leaned back in his chair and chuckled. 'I'm glad to see your spirit revived,' he remarked. 'But I am quite serious, Mrs Pickering. You must look to the future; you cannot mourn loved ones for ever, no matter how much you cared for them.'

Judging the interview to be over, Patricia busied herself in gathering up her gloves and the leather satchel in which she kept her papers. It was true she had loved her father deeply and still missed him terribly. But her husband? Well, naturally she missed him — but love? Somehow Patricia had come to think of being in love as an unnecessary extravagance that had nothing to do with her way of life; more to do with knights and ladies from a bygone age.

And even then, love and passion was for the dreams of young, inexperienced ladies — not for her.

Surely — not for her.

* * *

Lord Percy Alexander, along with his estate manager Mr Fairbrass, had ridden into Wakefield before noon.

After partaking of a jar of beer and a light luncheon at The Weaver's Arms their ways had parted; Fairbrass to attend to some business at the corn chandler's, and Percy to meet up with an old acquaintance. They were to reassemble at the solicitor's rooms at three of the clock.

'It's a little late of the hour, but Standish's clerk assures me that he has only one appointment after noon and it should be completed by three,' Fairbrass had informed him.

'Excellent,' replied Percy who had by now examined the north field, agreed its lack of worth for development, and was interested to establish how much revenue could be expected by its sale.

He spent a convivial hour with an old friend from Oxford who was passing through Wakefield on his way to Leeds, and was putting up at The King's Head. Unfortunately, however, the shared reminisces took rather longer to discuss than Percy had anticipated and consequently he arrived in the vicinity of Standish solicitors practice feeling hot and dishevelled.

He paused on the doorstep in an attempt to straighten the knot in his neck-cloth and then remove a patch of mud which he spied clinging to his highly polished boots. A gentleman should always look the part, more especially a newly impoverished gentleman. He took a handkerchief from his pocket and with a hand on the oak door for support, balanced on one leg in order to polish the mud from the boot.

Unexpectedly the door opened and before he could collect himself, Percy found his face thrust against a young and comely bosom.

'My word,' stammered Percy, recovering himself with all speed and lifting his face to a more upright position. 'I do beg pardon, ma'am.' He looked up into a pair of wide, startled eyes, the colour of which put him in mind of a stormy sea.

'My goodness,' said Patricia, steadying herself against a broad and manly chest — then, on meeting a pair of warm, brown eyes speckled with amber in their depths, rapidly taking a backward step.

'My goodness,' she repeated. 'I'd have thought it a little early, sir, to be falling down drunk.'

Percy's eyes crinkled to a smile. 'Indeed, I can understand your thinking so, but do assure you only a veritable drop of ale has passed my lips. Overbalanced. Not even a trifle disguised — do assure you. Dashed awkward. Do apologise — most profusely. Don't know quite what happened. One moment I was leaning on the door in an effort to make myself presentable before entering these premises — the next . . . '

'Oh?' said Patricia, an answering smile pulling at the corner of her lips. 'Presentable? Well, if you will allow me, sir . . . ' She deftly brushed his shoulder free of an imaginary speck of dirt. 'That should do the trick. You are now impeccable. The cat's whiskers. Think nothing of frightening a poor, fragile woman half to death in your pursuit for perfection — I pray you won't allow it to weigh with you in the least. Good afternoon sir.'

Percy turned to watch her elegant figure as it retreated down the street, an expression of baffled incredulity on his face.

My word. What a wonderful-looking woman. His heart fluttered absurdly in his chest. Her eyes. Had they been blue or green? Whatever their colour, they'd been glorious. And her body: he'd only brushed against it for a moment. A moment of perfumed softness, of sweetness; a moment of — well, to put it frankly — magic.

'My word,' said Percy wonderingly, aloud, as he continued to gaze after her. Who would have thought to find a woman like that in Wakefield?

In a trance-like manner he continued through the small vestibule and into the outer office of Standish's premises where he found Fairbrass seated on one of the chairs lining the room, studying a periodical.

'Fairbrass.' Lord Percy Alexander

nodded to his estate manager.

'My lord?' Fairbrass glanced up and rose to his feet. 'Ah, now you're here, we can go straight in. Standish is quite ready for us — ' He stopped abruptly and examined Percy a little more closely. 'Forgive me for asking, sir, but — are you quite well?'

'Ain't foxed, if that's what you mean.' Percy gave himself a shake and hoped his expression wasn't as glazed as he suspected it might be. 'I'm perfectly well, Fairbrass — perfectly. Who was that lady?'

'Lady, sir? Which lady?'

'Don't pretend that you didn't see her, man. My God, how ever could you not have noticed her?'

It was the turn of Fairbrass to look bemused. 'Oh yes, I did see a young lady take her leave.'

'Did you? Fine figure of a woman, I thought . . . Indeed — dashed near knocked her off her feet . . . Be a good chap, find out who she is. Like to apologise in some way.'

'Apologise, my lord?'

'Begged pardon at the time, naturally. But, even so — can't go round knocking people off their feet in that manner. Not the done thing — eh?'

'Just so, my lord,' said Fairbrass, raising an eyebrow before following Percy into the solicitor's inner sanctum.

After the civilities had been performed, the gentlemen sat down. But before they proceeded to business, Percy leaned forward impatiently, able to contain his interest no longer.

'A lady just left your office. Dark-haired, neat-featured; bonnet — grey, I think. Elegant bearing. D'you have her name?'

Briefly, he wondered if he had appeared a little too eager; Standish was gazing at him in a slightly perplexed manner. Percy ran his fingers round the inside of his neck-cloth. 'Feel as though I should know her, that's all. Might have been introduced at some time and misremembered her name.'

Fairbrass gave a small cough.

'Oh,' said Standish. 'Of course. You must mean Mrs Pickering.'

Percy said nothing. Well, he might have known a lady of her ilk would be well and truly married. Bound to be, really. Figure like that. Smile like that. Eyes that almost took his breath from his body.

Dimly he became aware of Standish's voice.

'Now in what way may I be of assistance to you my lord?'

'Ah yes — to business,' said Percy. 'Hardly noticed her really.'

3

Spring had come in fits and starts this year, awakening in Patricia a restlessness and a wildness of spirit that made her uncomfortable with herself. When spring eventually slipped its long days into a disappointingly cold May, she felt as though somehow she had missed something. As though — whatever that elusive something was — it had gone now and was far out of reach.

The ventures she'd made into society now her mourning period was over had turned out to be regrettably dull. She'd attended musical evenings, and accepted invitations to afternoon tea and dinner at the vicarage. She'd even been to a ball, where she had been appalled to find herself seated with a crowd of chaperones discussing the likely marriage prospects of their charges. She had left the gathering as soon as she decently could.

If it were not for her riding, her charity work, the lending library, and her frequent forays on foot about the town, she felt she would go quite mad. Sometimes when she was out walking, in a purposeful manner which belied the fact that often she had no real objective, she would fancy she glimpsed the strong set of shoulders and the loose-limbed stride of someone she knew — yet did not know, and would remember with a smile the moment when she found herself struck off balance, by a strange young aristocrat on the steps of John Standish's office.

That the young man was not of her world, she'd known at a glance. But nevertheless, she would allow herself to remember for a moment the wide humorous mouth and the warm brown eyes; the admiration in them as his gaze swept over her from head to toe. He had been every inch the charming, pleasure-seeking young aristocrat and had probably never done a day's work in his life.

Pushing him from her thoughts,

Patricia allowed herself to acknowledge the fact that, for the first time in her life, she was bored. Even though her time of official bereavement was over and she was accepting invitations again, the hours fell all too heavily in the day.

Never in all of her twenty-six years had Patricia felt so without purpose. Since the age of fourteen, when her mother had died, she had helped her father in the office and had proved early on how capable she was with figures and accounting. Furthermore, she had enjoyed the task, and hated being away from the mill even for the shortest of times. Up until the time of her marriage, the Flint mill had been her life. And even after her marriage, she had assisted in bringing the Pickering mill up to date, with new machinery and ways of working which were less arduous for the workers and more productive for the mill.

Since the deplorable scene three months ago, when Robert had proposed marriage, she had endeavoured to avoid meeting him. Nevertheless she had come across him once by accident at the livery stables they both frequented. He had been a little subdued at first and, feeling sorry for him, Patricia had ridden along with him for a while.

But once again, as soon as they were out of sight of the other riders, Robert started with an apology for pressing his suit — recognising that he'd been perhaps a little precipitate, and that of course he should have realised she needed time for consideration, but he was sure that her good sense would eventually prevail upon her to accept his offer.

Of course she had refused him again, and from that time on had taken even greater care to keep out of his way and avoid going near the Flint mill.

Only now did she realise how much of her life had been spent in thinking about the business, even when not actively taking part in the day-to-day running of it. Only now did she wonder whether she had in fact done the right thing in selling Pickering and alienating herself from the Flint mill. Surely someone, more intelligent than she, would have found a way to hold an interest that meant her visiting the mills from time to time. But marriage to her cousin would have been too high a price to pay.

Marriage to Robert? No — never that.

So she had done what she felt her father would have wanted; what her husband would have expected, as they'd had no children. She'd sold Pickering's, continued to hold an interest in Flint's and now she had no recourse but to play at becoming a lady.

After all, it was what her father had most wished for her. The only disagreement that had ever taken place between them had been over his desire for her to attend an academy for young ladies.

Eventually, albeit sullenly, she had bent to his will and at the age of sixteen travelled to London with her father and been deposited at the academy, which promised instruction in deportment, manners and social abilities. Once there, she had learned to iron out her vowels — to say *bun* instead of boon, and *grarse* instead of grass. She was also to learn to walk with a book on her head, arrange flowers, write answers to invitations of a social nature, and either take up watercolour painting or learn to ride side-saddle. Since she'd only ever driven a carriage and pair, and had no talent for painting, the riding seemed to be the lesser of the two evils.

Directly she arrived back in Wakefield six months on, however, her life was once again so busy that she forgot about the riding. But now, years later and with time hanging heavy on her hands, she remembered the feeling of freedom she had felt in cantering in the London parks, and had the sudden notion to take it up again.

Despite it being frowned upon for a woman to do so, Patricia usually chose to ride alone. This morning her neat but curvaceous figure was clothed in a new dark blue riding habit made of the finest merino wool. Her taste in clothes was always understated, well-tailored and fashioned in the one thing she knew about — cloth of the very finest quality. Now she was out of mourning, it would no longer cause a stir should she choose to wear brighter colours, but she rather liked the dark blue. With her dark, smooth hair, fair skin and unusually coloured eyes, she knew she suited the severely fitting riding habit to perfection, but the knowledge gave her little pleasure.

She was bored, bored, bored.

Moodily she hacked along the quiet lanes that skirted Wakefield on her chestnut mare, keeping close to the hawthorn hedges that divided the countryside. She met with very little traffic on this particular track, and it was a route she knew Robert never frequented as it was not particularly scenic. Patricia sighed and searched round for something — anything — to engage her interest. The field close by was used for grazing sheep, but there seemed to be no sheep on it at present. A little way off up the lane, there was a gate. Patricia eyed it speculatively. The grass on the other side of the hedge looked inviting for a gallop. The gate looked — well, almost derelict.

It wouldn't take much just to nudge it open.

Law-abiding at heart, Patricia glanced over her shoulder before dismounting and with one hefty push, swung the gate wide. Gleefully she led her horse through into the field, pulling the gate to — but not using a latch to fix it, for there was none.

At first she cantered the perimeter of the field. Her mount responded happily enough, but on arrival back at the gate Patricia, gaining confidence, decided to take a diagonal path across to the far corner. She felt the rush of wind in her hair and the thud of hoofs echoed the steady beating of her heart. Giving a sudden laugh, she kicked her horse's sides and urged her forwards, feeling at last — after all these months of sadness — the exuberance of being alive.

The sensation evaporated however as she turned her mount in a slow curve, set her to canter again; then let her eyes search out the gate, for leaning over it in a nonchalant manner, was the figure of a young man.

Fiddlesticks, thought Patricia. But why should she care? He probably had no more right to be here than she had.

She looked again, then slowed her horse to a trot for there was something about him that caused her pulses to race even faster and a sweat to break out on her forehead.

* * *

Percy had been walking the estate since dawn. Every morning for the past two weeks, weather permitting, he'd donned buckskins, a light nankeen jacket and old top boots and set out in a different direction. Slowly, in large sweeping circles, he was rediscovering the more accessible reaches of the estate. Not just the immediate estate, but the outlying fields and pastures, places he'd hardly looked at in detail since he was a boy. At first he'd regarded his explorations as a necessary chore, but the more he walked and the more he explored, the more his interest grew.

At first he was dismayed by the sheer extent of the work to be done, but as he'd gone on with his investigations making neat, precise records as he went, he'd discovered a certain pride in his and his forebear's work, and then the sudden urgent need to do better; to make up for the neglect of recent years, and make the living here prosperous and good.

In accordance with his plans he'd spent the spring early season in London, but found to his considerable surprise that he missed Yorkshire; missed the dales and the work he was doing with Fairbrass. He'd even missed looking over the fig-ures and wishing they told a different story, for although the lambing had gone well, the estate was still in dire need of funds. In short; he missed his home.

Although he had gone to London with a purpose, he had signally failed to follow the purpose through. Somehow or other, although Percy didn't really believe in love of the romantic kind, he found it difficult to consider a marriage without a fair amount of at least *liking* involved. *Stands to reason,* he thought to himself defiantly. *If you're going to share a marriage bed — and a lot of other things as well — you've got to at least like each other.*

He'd had in mind someone jolly-looking. Someone perhaps slim, with dark hair and a comely bosom. Someone with greyish, stormy eyes that held a twinkle in their depths. Someone, say, like Mrs Pickering. But he'd found no-one remotely like Mrs Pickering amongst the miss-ish, blushing, rich young debutants on their coming-out.

Wishing that he didn't think about Mrs Pickering quite so often, Percy paused to take a slug of water from his stoneware bottle and leaned on one of his decrepit old gates. *Not even a latch on this one*, Percy thought disapprovingly and made a note. *No sheep here either. Why not? Perfectly good grazing land!* He made another note.

Then at the sound of hoof-beats, he looked up.

Hardly daring to believe the scene before him, he watched as the rider came towards him, reined in her horse and looked down at him out of astonished eyes. Wide eyes that were startlingly familiar to him, were neither grey nor quite blue, and held a hint of amusement in their expression.

Percy straightened and removed his hat. 'Good morning, Mrs Pickering,' he said with a mock bow.

The lady gave a half smile and nodded. 'You have the advantage on me, sir. I do not recall exchanging names at our last meeting.'

'Name's Percy Alexander. Beg you won't hold it against me. My friends call me Percy.'

Lord Percy Alexander!

Patricia swallowed. Of course she'd heard the name. Dimly she was aware at the time of her husband's death that the old Lord James Alexander of Wakefield Hall had also died, leaving two sons and a daughter. She even recalled briefly feeling sorry for them, but then quickly reminding herself that children of the aristocracy were brought up by servants in the main, and would not feel a parental loss in quite the same way as the rest of the human race would.

She looked down at him now from her high perch on the chestnut's back and saw that the boyish looks and manner were overshadowed by dark patches round his eyes and a crease of worry in his forehead. Immediately her sympathy was stirred.

'Should I call you 'my lord'?' she asked uncertainly.

Lord Percy gave an attractive grin. 'No need for that, Mrs Pickering. Regard you as my friend. Be pleased if you'd call me Percy.'

Although on the occasion of their last meeting he'd hardly uttered a word, she realised with a shock that she'd remembered his voice too, his abrupt staccato style of speech and the laugh he often tossed off at the end of a sentence which somehow softened it. She stared into his eyes — brown but with specks of amber — and found it difficult to look away.

Suddenly she came to her senses; surely she shouldn't still be sitting in saddle, with her horse munching at the grass, and the gate that proclaimed she was trespassing, closed between them?

Unhooking her knee from the saddle's pommel, she slid gracefully from the chestnut's back. Percy held the gate open and made a great business of shutting it after her.

'My first name is Patricia. How do you know my last?' she asked, her curiosity getting the better of her.

Lord Percy flushed slightly. 'Asked Standish,' he answered without preamble. 'Apologise for nearly knocking

51

you off your feet when we met. Pure accident — assure you. Wanted to know who you were. Wanted to apologise properly.'

Patricia smiled. 'You did so at the time, I remember — and most handsomely. The fault was hardly yours alone. If I had not been so very out of temper at the time and in such a rush to get away, I would not have wrenched at the door in such haste — and then the whole incident would never have taken place.'

Lord Percy raised an eyebrow. 'Had you had bad news, then, Mrs Pickering? At Standish's offices — I mean.'

She shrugged. 'Hardly that. My father had died some fifteen months previously — then my husband shortly after, but, well, I'd decided to sell the Pickering mill so as not to be in competition with my cousin who now owns half the Flint mill. There were still papers to be signed and, well, various things to be cleared up.'

'Ah,' said Lord Percy giving an

unexpected smile.

They fell into step side by side, and Patricia realised that without her even noticing, Lord Percy had taken the reins from her and was gently but firmly walking her horse. Surely that was rather presumptuous, even for a lord? She supposed that the correct thing for her to do would be to thank him for his help and then continue her ride at a pace he couldn't match. Yes, that would surely be the correct and sensible thing to do.

'You are a widow, then, Mrs Pickering?'

'So it would seem. And you are the new Lord of Wakefield Hall and therefore owner of much that we survey?'

'So it would seem,' Lord Percy echoed with a sigh.

'Are the responsibilities so great that you must sigh, then, sir?'

'No! Well, yes, sometimes,' he admitted. 'I might have inherited a title and an ancestral home, but there's also my father's debts to contend with and I have the legacy of a rundown estate, which,' he tapped his notebook, 'I am trying to get the measure of now. Not to mention a couple of siblings whose welfare is my responsibility.'

They walked a little further and the chestnut gave an impatient shake of her head at a cloud of passing insects.

'I see,' said Patricia eventually. 'But it also seems to me that you love your home, and your father's debts are hardly your fault. I should think what lies ahead for you might be looked upon as a stimulating challenge. Better, anyway, than the life of tedium I have to endure.'

She met his eyes fearlessly. The expression in them was surprised, but not unpleasantly so.

'The question begs, then, Mrs Pickering — if you find yourself to be bored, why did you sell your husband's mill?'

Patricia gave a laugh which she was dismayed to hear came out as a very unladylike snort. 'Only a man could ask that question . . . It may have escaped your notice but a woman running a mill is no common thing. Besides, I have enough trouble with Robert as it is.'

'Robert? Ah, your young son; a health problem, perhaps?'

Patricia sighed. 'No, unfortunately I'm not lucky enough to have children. No indeed, Robert is my cousin. He owns half the Flint mill. I own the other half and he has taken it into his head to think that it would be a wonderful thing indeed if we were to marry.'

There was a silence long enough for Patricia to comprehend how very inappropriate it was for her to have confided her business quite so openly on so short an acquaintance.

Lord Percy's voice, when he finally spoke, sounded perfectly measured and controlled. 'Sounds like a thoroughly sensible suggestion to me.'

'I suppose it would do — to a man.'

'Forgive my saying, but you're a young woman, Mrs Pickering — still plenty of time to have children. Why not marry and still be part of the life you love, with all its challenges?'

Patricia gave another sigh, this one verging on the impatient. 'You're overlooking one little thing. To do that, I should have to marry Robert. And in so doing I'd also lose control of my shares in the Flint mill.'

Biting her lip, she looked away. 'The reason my father left me a part interest was so that I could temper any of Robert's more ridiculous extravagances and protect our workers. I still carry a vote on all major decisions ... Anyway, I do not wish to marry Robert — I can't bring myself to even like him. And where a marriage is concerned I feel strongly that one needs to at least like one's partner.'

Lord Percy stopped walking and gazed at her intently. The sun came out from behind a cloud, and somewhere Patricia heard a skylark singing.

'What is it?' she asked, staring back and for some reason finding it was quite difficult to breathe.

'Mrs Pickering,' he said abruptly.

'Couldn't agree more. My word! Just come back from London myself. Felt it was time I was settling down — thought I'd look round for a bride up there — the season, y'know. Besides, need some extra blunt — not to put too fine a point on it . . . '

He sighed. 'Fool's errand. There they were, the so-called catches of the season. Don't call it the marriage mart for nothing y'know. Fortunes galore, pretty too, most of them . . . '

Absently, he patted the chestnut's neck and allowed his eyes to scan the landscape around them. 'Didn't inspire a spark of interest — not a spark. Tried to picture some of them in my mind — up here at Wakefield Hall . . . Couldn't seem to manage it. Insipid misses, from what I could see. Couldn't interest myself in their conversation at all — y'know?' He switched his attention back to Patricia. 'Didn't really like any of them.'

Forcing herself to look away from his animated expression, Patricia turned and glanced over the sparse hawthorn hedge as they continued to walk up the lane.

'That was your field, wasn't it? The one I was riding in? That makes me a trespasser. I'm sorry.'

Shrugging his shoulders, he smiled. 'It's all right. Just wondered what you were doing there, that's all — before I recognised you. If you ride for pleasure, there is plenty more interesting a vista to visit.'

'I was avoiding Robert. I know where he rides and have been unfortunate enough to come across him in the past. Every time I set eyes on him, it seems he must ask me to marry him again. It transpires I must skulk around in lesser-known lanes in order to avoid him for the rest of my life.'

'Either that,' murmured Lord Percy, uncharacteristically slowly. 'Or — marry somebody else.'

He stopped again and examined her very intently indeed.

'Mrs Pickering,' he said. 'Would you

consider marrying me?'

Wordlessly, Patricia stared back at him.

'Don't you see? It would solve all our problems, and the fact is — I do like you, Mrs Pickering, I really do.'

4

Stunned, Patricia took several moments to gather her wits. 'You are surely funning, sir!' she finally managed to say.

Lord Percy took a step back, but his eyes remained steady.

'No; I was never more serious in my life.'

For a moment Patricia believed him, and a feeling of wonderment washed over her. Then common sense prevailed.

'But you can't — you can't want to marry me.'

'Don't see why on earth not. Good-looking woman — thought so the first time I met you.'

'But I'm — I'm only the daughter of a mill owner. I have some money, true, but not enough to pay off your father's gambling debts, I'll warrant. And even if I did — why should I?'

A shadow passed over his face. 'I apologise, Mrs Pickering. Hadn't thought you might not like the idea of marrying me. Of course, would never expect you to pay off my father's debts. Glad to say, part way through doing that already and the banks are now convinced of my good intentions and prepared to be more patient than I first thought.

'No, it's the estate that needs money if it's not to go to rack and ruin. And of course once the initial money's been spent, it's self-perpetuating. Nothing wrong with the estate a quick injection of cash won't fix. Give you my word.'

He looked away at the surrounding fields for a moment, then back at Patricia. 'I thought — that is, wondered — if perhaps you would consider it a good investment to join forces with me so that — in time to come — our children could reap the benefits. It would be a partnership. A civil contract.'

A sudden smile lit up his face as he warmed to his theme. 'You'd no longer have to worry about your cousin Robert;

you'd have a home, a position in society, the advantages and freedoms that a widow of a mill owner — respectable though that is — would never experience. Social standing, you know. See your children — *our* children — reap the benefits.'

He broke off with a crooked smile. 'Said that before, didn't I?'

In spite of her confusion, Patricia found herself struggling not to laugh out loud. 'Forgive me, my lord. It isn't personal, you understand — the whole notion is just so nonsensical. You sir, are destined to marry a lady.'

'You're a lady, ain't you?' countered Lord Percy with another surprisingly sweet smile. 'If you're not,' he glanced down at her neat figure, 'you're a master of disguise.'

Trying not to be swayed by the sheer unexpectedness of the position she found herself in, by the craziness of the idea, and the undoubted charm of the eager young man before her, Patricia struggled to keep a realistic grip on the situation. She took a long breath, smoothed her skirts and focused her attention on Lord Percy's left eyebrow which, seemingly independently of its master's wishes, had a habit of raising itself.

'You know very well what I mean, sir.' The eyebrow went up a notch. 'You know nothing about me. I know nothing about you . . . We move in very different social circles. Oh, the very idea is nothing but a hum.'

There was a long silence during which Patricia became aware of the approach of a farm wagon. The man driving it touched his hat as he passed. Silently she watched its lumbering progress as far as the bend in the lane.

'Assure you, madam, I'm no hoaxer . . . Well, certainly not at the moment; not now. Dashed bad form to ask for a lady's hand in marriage as a jest.'

This truly was bizarre. She wanted to laugh; wanted to cry. She had to leave — now — immediately, before the whole idea got totally out of hand. How desperate must Lord Percy be to consider a marriage to the daughter of one mill owner and the widow of another? Everyone knew the aristocracy only married into trade as a last resort, and someone with Lord Percy's advantages could take his pick of England's heiresses.

Patricia looked up. His eyes were smiling down at her. They were most attractive eyes. Indeed, if she gazed at them for too long, her mind threatened to cease functioning.

'Do you have an answer for me?'

Before she could stop it, a wistful sigh escaped her. Hurriedly she straightened her shoulders and became businesslike. It was, after all, a business proposition.

'Sir, I'm mindful of the compliment you pay me, but pray consider. Our circumstances are so very different. This is a mere whim on your part. I must only surmise that, after due consideration, you'll acknowledge the plan to be as foolhardy as do . . .'

She broke off as Lord Percy turned

quickly away. 'Apologise again,' he said from the side of his mouth. 'Didn't intend to insult you or upset you, Mrs Pickering. Last thing on my mind. Thought we'd deal well together, but daresay I'm not such a good marriage prospect after all.'

Patricia swallowed. She had glimpsed the hurt in his eyes. Before she'd thought about it, her hand had found its way to rest on his sleeve.

'I'm sorry, too,' she said softly. 'And I am truly flattered, but . . . '

Lord Percy wheeled round on his heel to face her again.

'Mrs Pickering, please believe me when I say I am serious in this proposal. Never more so. Pockets to let, I make no secret of it. Couldn't afford to marry you if you were poor as a church mouse. Couldn't immediately support you — d'you see? The money from the mill would help set us on our feet again. Still be hard work. Won't be living in the lap of luxury — but plenty of sheep, plenty of wool. Estate's neglected but I mean to put that to rights and I will. Need the ideal woman beside me, that's all.

'No namby-pamby miss, but a good, strong, sensible lass, with a mind of her own — not frightened of a challenge or hankering after an extravagant life with the ton of society. Besides — told you before, Mrs Pickering. I like you.'

For a long, long moment their eyes locked and Patricia felt a curious sensation start in the fluttering of her heart and end somewhere in the region of her stomach.

'I like you too,' she admitted breathlessly.

Lord Percy covered the gloved hand on his sleeve with his own tanned bare fingers. They lingered for a moment on the naked skin of her wrist. Patricia shivered at their touch.

'Like you to think about it,' he said. 'I will, too, although — do assure you — I won't change my mind. Talk to Standish about me if you've a mind. I'll be here next week, whatever may befall.

Promise you that, Mrs Pickering. At this time — by the gate.' He nodded in the direction they had come from. 'You can give me your final answer then and I vow I'll abide by it.'

Patricia watched as though in a dream as he gently turned her horse for her. He indicated she put her booted foot into his hands before he hoisted her lightly into the saddle.

'Now go home, Mrs Pickering,' he instructed, 'and think on it.'

★   ★   ★

Percy watched as Patricia Pickering slowly walked her horse out of sight.

She didn't look back. Was that a good sign, or bad?

He suddenly realised he was gripping his notebook extremely tightly and, in an effort to still the pounding of his heart, he examined the last entry about a field with an unlatched, broken gate that was not being used for grazing.

Patricia Pickering. Far too much

alliteration to the name. Patricia Alexander — now that had an elegant ring to it. Lady Patricia Alexander sounded better still.

Fairbrass had been correct, he decided suddenly. Marriage with a local Yorkshire lass would be just the thing. So, she wasn't a member of the aristocracy; what difference should that make? She was intelligent, attractive and had money — maybe not so very much as he would have liked, but the profits from selling a successful mill would be considerable.

Besides — he liked her.

Deciding he'd done enough walking for today, he took the fastest route home and immediately set about commissioning Fairbrass to arrange an appointment with Standish as soon as may be.

'I'm sure, sir, should the matter be urgent, an immediate visit would not be called into question,' said Fairbrass. 'Perhaps it's a matter you would care to discuss with me first?'

'No, Fairbrass, I most assuredly would not,' said Percy with one of his sudden firm smiles which his estate manager had come to realise brooked no argument.

So it was that less than two hours later, Percy was facing John Standish across his desk.

He came to the point without preamble. 'Like to know as much as possible about a client of yours. A Mrs Patricia Pickering. Believe she sold a mill recently and also has part ownership in the Flint mill. Believe we might have done business with them in the past via my estate manager Fairbrass.'

Standish cleared his throat. 'My lord,' he started. 'You will understand that Mrs Pickering and, indeed, her late father Mr Flint are old standing clients and I cannot discuss their business out of hand . . . '

'Understand that, Standish. Of course I do. I've had reason to meet Mrs Pickering recently — socially, you comprehend . . . One or two things she mentioned concerned me. She has a cousin, Robert I believe she called him, who appears to be making a nuisance of himself in trying to press his suit. I can't quite like that state of affairs, Standish. How long has Mrs Pickering been widowed?'

'Quite some fourteen months now, sir. Her father died only six months before her husband's sudden death of heart failure.'

'Only just out of mourning then, isn't she — eh? But he's been badgering her for months?'

'So I understand. It's only fair, sir, to draw to your attention the fact that Mr Robert Flint is also my client. I endeavour to serve the both of them to the best of my ability.'

'Does that include, Standish, advising her in any decisions of a matrimonial nature?'

'No indeed. I would never presume.'

'It strikes me, Standish, that a woman of Mrs Pickering's age, or rather I should say of her youth and temperament, would be much better off in the marriage state.'

A spark of comprehension ignited in Standish's expression but he said nothing, merely rested his chin on his steepled fingers.

'What of the late Mr Pickering? Was he also one of your clients?'

Standish nodded. 'Felix Pickering, yes. A very unassuming gentleman. Softly spoken, well-educated and mannered. Astute, though, even though often short of breath and fragile. Of course now it's realised that his poor health was due to a condition of the heart. But it was a pleasure to do business with him, and his father before him.'

Thoughtfully, Percy stood up and walked to the bow-fronted window. Clasping his hands behind his back, he looked out over the street. He wondered about Patricia; wondered what business he had here, scrounging round for information, for any titbit of material he might use in order to persuade her to accept him.

He turned and sat down again.

'D'you think she's happy, Standish?'

If Standish felt surprise he managed to hide it. Nevertheless he looked at Percy for several moments before replying.

'Mrs Pickering is a lady who has always been fully occupied. I don't think I am betraying a confidence when I explain to you that on not having the family she desired, she put all her energies into the Pickering mill and was instrumental in its success. If she had been a man, she would have continued in the management of the mill and also since her father's death had a considerable influence in running the Flint mill.

'Happily the lady is left in a fortunate position; she does not have to marry anyone in order to survive, and is only likely to marry again in order to have the family she would so dearly love. I don't think there is anything more I can add to that.'

'Thank you, Standish. You have told me nothing that the lady herself has not informed me of, but I thank you anyway. In not answering my question, I know that I am right. The lady is far from happy — she is bored.'

He got to his feet as he spoke and held out his hand. 'Most obliged to you, Standish. Good afternoon.'

5

The next week seemed like an eternity to Patricia. Naturally, even if he did keep the appointment, she would have to refuse him. Again; for she had already done so — how many times? At least twice at his time of asking. Oh, it was all a nonsense!

But then there was the haunting memory of the touch of his fingers brushing the vulnerable patch of naked skin on the inside of her wrist. Her face heated up at the recollection. In retrospect, the touch had been so fleeting as to be non-existent — then why should it burn so in her memory?

By the dawning of the third day Patricia felt unable to bear her restlessness a moment longer and found herself driving her open carriage and pair out beyond Wakefield, west towards Dewsbury, and then climbing north in the direction of Leeds and Bradford.

By now she was used to the forests of chimney mills that rose from the valley floors creating a new landscape of prosperity for the area, but from the unaccustomed height of the top road, the sight was even more awe-inspiring. The old cottage industries of spinning and weaving wool were dying out, their place being taken by new machinery and mills which drew their power from the fast-flowing streams of the Pennines. But alongside all this new industrial growth she knew that farms were still thriving, and there were many thousands of sheep being grazed that provided the fleeces for the woollen mills. She also knew that many of these farms belonged to the large estate of Wakefield Hall — as did most of the sheep.

As she journeyed further to the north-west, climbing all the while, she attended her surroundings more closely, noticing with some concern that some of the villages she passed showed signs of neglect. Many of the cottage roofs appeared dilapidated and the dry-stone walls and the occasional barn also revealed tendencies for disrepair.

Patricia clicked her tongue. Looking at her surroundings with fresh eyes, she could see there was much to be done. Remembering Lord Percy's resolute expression as he'd vowed to improve the estate, she smiled a little and wondered if he would be giving orders to others or actually working alongside his men to rectify past wrongs.

Somehow, even on such little acquaintance, she knew she'd have to revise her earlier opinion that he'd never done a hard day's work in his life.

Finally, she reached her destination, which was nearly half way to the summit of a flat-topped limestone hill that had been pointed out to her on her ascent by a passing farm worker. Patricia looked around her. The air was fresh with the tang of the moors and she breathed in deeply and appreciatively. After drawing to a halt opposite the entrance to a long overgrown drive, she looked to its end and beheld a view of a grand Queen Anne-style mansion built of mellow York-stone.

Wakefield Hall in all its majesty!

Impossible to see from here its exact state of repair, but from this distance it looked to be sound of structure; large enough to be impressive yet not too imposing. It was a symmetrical building of three storeys with a separate stable block of goodly proportions.

Patricia clicked her tongue again. The drive should be cleared, the avenue of trees pruned and the side shrub areas cut back. Slowly, she manoeuvred her vehicle to travel on outside the dry-stone boundary wall, eventually stopping at a gate where a rosy-cheeked child sat munching on an apple.

She smiled at her and the little girl, solemn at first, suddenly gave an answering smile of such angelic bright-ness that Patricia's heart quite turned over. Then the child slid from the gate and ran away, calling to her mother to come look at the carriage.

There it was — that ache in her heart again.

She didn't take the time to tarry. Instead she clicked her tongue to her horses and drove on as though she had important business to attend to.

Lord Percy wanted children, he'd made that clear. She also wanted children, but with a hunger that sometimes made her body yearn. She was barely twenty-six, and knew there was still time to meet and marry someone new and have a whole brood of beautiful children — of course there was.

But she wanted children now; she didn't want to wait. Didn't want the long drawn-out process of putting herself on the marriage mart; finding a suitable suitor, taking part in a courtship and complying with all the accompanying unwritten rules and regulations. She sighed impatiently. The conventional route could take years.

She travelled another four miles and still all she surveyed seemed to belong to the Alexander estate. Turning southwards once again with a small sigh, she straightened her spine and squared her shoulders. This time as she passed the Queen Anne mansion, she kept her horses' pace smart. What had she been thinking of to make this journey, to consider even for the smallest of moments that this mad idea might be feasible? Not only was Lord Percy Alexander a member of the aristocracy, he was a landowner; he was, in every way possible, her superior. Just because he was also personable and the proposition he put before her attractive to a woman of her capabilities, did not mean for an instant that it was possible.

A marriage between them was clearly, totally inconceivable.

* * *

While for Patricia the week moved inordinately slowly, Percy found that the days went all too fast.

He endeavoured to go about his

estate business in his normal manner, and if Fairbrass noted an increase in his usual nervous energy he refrained from comment.

Percy still walked every morning in his large sweeping circles. Occasionally he went alone, but more often was accompanied by a couple of the Irish wolfhounds for which his father and Wakefield Hall were famous. By the end of the week, although he had far from covered the whole of the inner estate, which comprised some five hundred acres of farmland and the same amount of woodland and grazing, he had a far wider knowledge of the magnitude of the task before him. He'd visited his tenant farmers, made notes of their immediate needs, listed the outlying villages and the amenities they contained, and taken a long hard-nosed look at which cottage craft industries were self-sufficient enough to continue in the face of the industrial revolution that was taking place.

'My father was not sufficiently

abreast of things,' he confided to Fairbrass. 'Not saying we're to change our ways completely, but we must move with the times, eh?'

'I couldn't agree more, sir. But some caution is required if we require the co-operation of the people — particularly the tenant farmers.'

'Naturally. I'll consult them at every turn. Always give them a say, eh?'

Fairbrass nodded and walked away with a lighter step, because the new young Lord Percy Alexander was turning out to be a man after his own heart.

Almost subconsciously, Percy found he was making lists of assets he might use in order to plead his case with Patricia. Everywhere he went on the estate, he tried to picture what Patricia might see and make of the scene before her. Somehow, he hadn't really noticed the interior of Wakefield Hall for many years. He suddenly became uncomfortably aware of the shabby curtains, the well-worn carpets and the general air of fading grandeur around him. He shrugged his shoulders. There was little he felt he could do about it.

He toured the walled kitchen garden and discussed with the head gardener the possibility of employing an extra boy to keep the plots weed-free, thereby increasing the yield. The produce was meant to feed the entire household and also to help the needy on the estate — and after all, he reasoned to himself, it should be cheap enough to run. Mentally he put a large tick in the asset column against 'kitchen garden', but left the space next to the interior of Wakefield Hall blank.

By the time the day of his appointed meeting with Patricia dawned, he had convinced himself that she would be happy to accept his proposal on the strength of all he had to offer her. She had enough sense to know it wasn't a love match. Good heavens, no, how could it be?

As she'd rightly pointed out, they hardly knew each other, and anyway he'd been completely plain with her and said that her inherited money would come in useful but she would naturally have a say in the spending of it. No, it was never a romantic proposition, certainly not; but she was past the age of caring about that sort of thing, and besides she had been married before.

Briefly Percy wondered what kind of a marriage it had been. That Patricia had worked together with her husband in order to improve the standards at the mill, he already knew. He pushed any queries about the nature of the rest of the marriage to one side as something he didn't need to know about.

Now that the initial exhilaration of his proposition had worn off, he thought about it calmly — logically, almost, as though he was investing in a new piece of equipment, rather like Jethro Tull's new seed drill.

She seemed strong — in a feminine way, of course. Not the sort of girl to shy at the first fence, not a shrinking violet to be forever clinging to his arm as though she daren't venture forth alone; not the sort to cause a scene either — she'd know how to behave in polite company all right, but he doubted she'd allow herself to be patronised just because she hadn't been born a lady.

She had a pleasant manner along with a well-modulated voice with only a small trace of the Yorkshire about it, and was just six months older than him. A good thing in a wife, he felt, to be round about the same age as the husband. Probably have the same ideas about things.

Yes, all in all, he decided to himself, the idea — impetuous though it might have been — had been basically sound. He gave a huge grin. It was a sensible idea. Possibly the most sensible idea he'd ever had in his life!

The day dawned bright and clear. Congratulating himself on his extreme level-headedness and having taken extra care with his toilet, but nevertheless feeling rather more nervous than he had anticipated, Percy set off with the two Irish wolfhounds at his heels.

He was there early. He leaned on the gate wondering if she would arrive by carriage, or on horseback; whether she would be wearing her severely tailored riding habit — which, incidentally, he'd noticed flattered her curves. Or perhaps — if she was using her carriage — she would be attired in a more feminine gown and a chip straw bonnet.

Not that it mattered what she chose to wear, as long as she came.

Time wore on. Maybe she wouldn't come.

No — that was unthinkable. She'd come, he was sure on it.

Percy walked as far as the corner of the lane and back again. Trying to ignore the sinking feeling making itself known in the pit of his stomach, he looked at the field Patricia had ridden across a week ago.

The pasture looked good. He knew now that the sheep that grazed there in the winter months were up in the hills for the summer, their coats newly shorn. With a wry smile, he wondered how long it would take him to learn all the ways of the country.

Then all thoughts stopped at the sound of approaching hoof-beats.

Was it her? It must be her.

Percy's mouth went dry and his heart suddenly started to thud quite painfully in his chest.

* * *

Cautiously, Patricia approached the gate where she could already see Lord Percy standing. With fingers that suddenly wouldn't do as they were bid, Patricia gathered the reins in one hand and prepared to dismount.

'You came,' he remarked with the disarming smile that Patricia had already come to know.

'As you see.' She looked down at him, remembered all over again what very attractive eyes he had, and struggled for her usual calm.

'Thank God. Thought you might not,' he said in a voice so full of relief that Patricia couldn't help grinning.

'Sorry, Mrs Pickering. My manners are quite forgot. Good day to you.' He pulled off his hat and stepped forward to assist her in her graceful slide from the saddle. 'You came,' he said again, this time with a break in his voice.

Patricia gave a light, shaky laugh. 'You said that already.'

His hands were firm around her waist as she dismounted. For a long moment their glances locked and held — their faces only inches apart.

At a stroke all Patricia's earlier resolve to refuse him, disappeared.

He looked so delighted to see her.

She felt so truly delighted to see him.

Eventually he released his hold on her.

'Realise now, Mrs Pickering,' he started, turning the brim of his hat in his fingers as he spoke. 'Realise now, it was a presumption on my part when you are still comparatively newly widowed and all — well, apologise if I took you by surprise. Have to admit — took myself by surprise, too.

'Seemed a good scheme, though. Still does. An excellent scheme. Been thinking about it — little else really . . . But, well . . . '

Is this really happening? thought Patricia, watching Percy struggling to make himself and his proposition clear. Percy, who was actually so very sweet, giving her the chance to turn him down while at the same time almost willing her to say yes, crazy though it was, to his proposal.

He had started to pace up and down now, still talking, still manhandling his poor hat. He was saying something about sheep and mending barns and not being able to stretch quite now to a honeymoon abroad, but would she be content with London — which wasn't at all bad at the end of summer, although, of course, they could just go to Richmond and go back to London later, for the little season perhaps, in autumn? Only that way they'd miss the shooting, which would be a pity . . .

Lord Percy stopped walking and looked at her.

She stared back.

'Quite understand,' he said suddenly. 'Quite understand if my way of life doesn't appeal. Quite see if you prefer to stay a widow; know you've all that is comfortable and you've no worries. Quite see it could be a restful life. Just thought you might like to — you know — marry me?'

'Oh, Lord Percy,' Patricia answered. 'I find myself without words. Yours is the sort of proposition girls only dream of. I came here intending to refuse you. I thought we were too different; that I could never be wife enough to run a big house and all the other things that go with the position . . . '

She stopped for a long moment; then looked straight back at him. 'But it's suddenly occurred to me that actually . . . Well, I dare say, that running

Wakefield Hall would be not so very different from running a mill . . . '

'A mill?' echoed Percy, his left eyebrow raising a notch.

'Well, I employed a mill manager, of course, after Felix died. But, make no mistake — I ran that mill for a lengthy time before selling. It's not accepted, you see, for a woman to run a mill, so I had to pretend. We all had to pretend, until I found a buyer . . . Anyway, this is beside the point.'

Lord Percy's smile broadened causing deep creases to show in his cheeks. 'Mrs Pickering — Patricia, does this mean you are prepared to accept my offer?'

She gave a tremulous smile. 'Well my lord — I mean — Percy, I think I'm capable of being a good wife to you, so I rather think it does!'

'I'll take good care to see that you never regret this,' he answered in a more sober tone.

Patricia swallowed. She must follow his lead and try to establish a more businesslike side to this conversation. There were certain issues and conditions she needed to make plain.

'I know of your circumstances already, of course,' she ventured. 'But only quite loosely.'

'Never tried to hide them — from you, at least. Pockets to let — well, not completely. But you won't find life at Wakefield Hall to be uncomfortable — assure you. I hope — that is, believe — we should deal well together.'

Patricia permitted herself another smile. 'Is that so, my lord? Forgive me, but marriage, for a woman, is a risky business.'

'Yet you desire a family?'

She felt her cheeks flush. 'I do. And it seems that despite my better judgement, marriage is therefore the only acceptable solution.'

The smile on Percy's lips died a little when he realised she was serious.

'So am I to be considered a 'solution' then?'

'Perhaps.'

His eyes narrowed. 'Our marriage would bring advantages — I promise. And I do believe we should suit.'

Now, watching as Percy endeavoured to make sense of the fact that although she'd accepted his offer there were still things she wished to discuss, Patricia wished she hadn't started this conversation. 'May I be frank with you?' she asked.

Lord Percy looked puzzled and a little fearful. 'Naturally.'

She took a deep breath. She hadn't intended this conversation, but suddenly at the sight of the young man in front of her, so happy at her acceptance of his unconventional proposal, she knew she could go no further without explaining matters.

'I fear . . . that there are certain areas of married life for which I do not have much aptitude.'

Lord Percy raised an eyebrow — the left one again, Patricia noticed quite inconsequentially. 'Such as?'

Feeling her colour heighten, she

turned away. 'I have told you that I should love to have children.'

Lord Percy nodded. 'As would I — as soon as you like.'

Patricia turned back to face him, her face flushed but her glance direct.

'I found I could not, did not, please my husband in that area.'

'Doesn't mean we should not be successful — together.'

'I have to explain — it wasn't only in the regard of not having children that I did not please him. I fear that there may be something about me that is amiss. My husband chose not to often share our marriage bed,' she finished in a small voice.

Lord Percy's eyebrow raised itself another notch but instead of looking serious and slightly disdainful as she'd imagined, he was smiling gently.

'Perhaps he wasn't in the petticoat line,' he suggested mildly. 'Pray give that particular notion no more thought, Mrs Pickering.'

'But suppose I cannot give you an

heir? I can't marry you under false pretences. You had to know.'

'And now I do. Good of you to tell me your fears, but let me say now that I disregard them totally. Besides, have a younger brother — he'll be my heir if I have no sons. You would still be provided for in that event — you have my word on that.'

A stricken feeling made itself felt under Patricia's ribs. 'I want, so much — so very much — to have a child with you. I'll do everything, anything in my power to make it happen.'

A sudden strong arm rested on her shoulder. Lord Percy pulled her soothingly against him. 'Don't upset yourself, m'dear. I'm judged to be good with horses . . .'

Patricia's lips twitched.

'Good with women, too.'

Her lips twitched some more.

He gave a small cough. 'Daresay we'll contrive between us.'

'Well, so long as you forebear from kicking me in the ribs and urging me to giddy up,' commented Patricia on the edge of a hysterical giggle.

A chuckle escaped him. 'That's better. A sense of humour is never amiss in the bedroom — we'll deal well together — I'm sure that we will. Thought so the first time I saw you. Never wrong about that sort of thing . . . I mean, not that I, well . . . Didn't mean exactly. Well not what you think I mean, of course, although, well, naturally one has . . . '

He broke off red-faced and Patricia gave a peal of laughter.

'Yes, I'm quite sure one has — but really, Percy, it's unnecessary to elucidate any further.'

'Quite,' said Percy with a cough.

Another laugh escaped her. 'I can't believe it,' she said. She turned to him, all her doubts and pent up feelings suddenly seeming unimportant. 'Is it really true? Are we really betrothed?'

Percy caught both her hands in his. 'We are,' he said. 'Now all that is to be done is to seal our bargain with a kiss.'

Expecting a chaste kiss, she leaned in towards him. At the first touch of his lips, closed but warm and gentle, she felt a fluttering inside herself quite new to her experience and, slightly frightened, she made to draw away.

Time stood still as she looked up into his hazel eyes. They still bore a light humorous expression, but with something else now stirring in their depths.

'Come, Mrs Pickering — think we can do better than that.'

He took one hand in his, nestling it against his chest. She could feel that his heart was beating as hard as her own. Then he wrapped his other arm close round her, and she felt safe, the emptiness inside her suddenly quietened, leaving only room for quite another kind of hunger. This time although the kiss started softly, almost like a whisper, as it went on it gathered in intensity, his lips suddenly harder against hers — tenderly probing for her response. With a small sigh she melted against him, her senses wanting no more than this moment — this feeling.

The delirious moment seemed to go on for ever, yet was over almost before it started.

He pulled away from her, his startled dark eyes looking into hers. 'My word,' said Percy, with a note of wonder in his voice. 'Mrs Pickering, I revise my earlier opinion. Consider we'll deal together *exceedingly* well!'

6

Many times over the next few weeks, Patricia had to pinch herself in order to believe she was awake.

It seemed that when the lord of the manor set his mind to doing something, all obstacles melted out of sight. A desire was no sooner expressed than fulfilled. Consequently plans went ahead at a speed which Patricia found amazing.

Neither of them wanted a large wedding, but it couldn't very well be a hole in the corner affair either. Eventually it was agreed that the banns be called immediately, allowing them to marry in the local church towards the end of June.

Lady Worthington, who had a country seat near York and was fortuitously Percy's godmother, had been appealed to by Percy to act as sponsor for Patricia. This state of affairs at first caused some degree of indignation on Patricia's part.

'It was never my intention to pretend to be something I am not,' she protested when Percy first mentioned the matter.

'Nor would I ask it of you,' replied Percy. 'Lady Worthington will smooth the way, that's all. Not asking you to pretend anything. You've worked on charitable missions — told me so yourself. Lady Worthington has only to drop your name in the right ear to have you at once established as being a valued acquaintance and charity worker, and gossip will do the rest.

'Besides, you'll be up to your ears in good works before you know it; believe me, she'll take every advantage of you once she knows your strengths for organisation.'

'Oh,' said Patricia, gratified. 'Well, if you put it like that . . . '

'I do put it like that,' said Percy. 'Can't have a story going round that we never set eyes on one another before I knocked you off your feet on a solicitor's doorstep now can we? No — better by far that Lady Worthington introduced us, no one can have anything to say to that. Chin up. Once we're married, everything will be right as a trivet.'

So saying, Lord Percy dropped a quick kiss on her nose and rushed off to sign final papers on the sale of the odd stretch of land which meant so little to him but fortunately so much to the rail company, and had been incidentally instrumental in the betrothed pair's true introduction.

Gazing at the ruby ring on her betrothal finger, Patricia was at one moment giddy with happiness, the next overset by anxieties that she was, perhaps, blinded by the idea of the life of privilege awaiting her, making too hasty a decision. But every time she set eyes on Percy, as she now called him, and his mouth widened into his spontaneously joyful smile, her lingering doubts fled away.

The least enjoyable time of this whirlwind betrothal period was the meeting with her cousin that John Standish arranged to take place at his office. John Standish himself had been delighted, if not as surprised as Patricia expected him to be, at the news of the betrothal.

'We have not gone into this on a whim,' Patricia explained to her father's old friend, whose opinion she respected. 'It's a sensible decision; he needs the support of someone like me. My experience in hard work and the organisation of a workforce will help us both . . . The estate is run down and needs new money to help set it to rights. And I, well, I will gain a good position and I think I'll enjoy organising such a large household and becoming acquainted with all of its dependants. Not so very different from running a mill, really.'

'You don't have to convince me. I consider it to be an excellent idea,' agreed Standish with a twinkle.

'Oh,' said Patricia slightly surprised that she didn't have to persuade him further. 'Well, good — that's good.'

Robert arrived at the solicitor's office punctually. He looked as handsome and well turned out as ever. His small linen white and crisp, his coat fitting to perfection; the bloodstone ring glinting on the finger of his elegant left hand.

'Congratulations, cousin,' he said with a curl to his lip. 'I understand now why you turned me down; you obviously had a richer prize in sight.'

Patricia flushed. 'No, Robert, you misunderstand. Lord Percy Alexander and I had not yet met when I refused your offer. However, I thank you for your felicitations.' The smile she gave him was answered with a disbelieving scowl, which she disregarded. 'Now Mr Standish will explain to you the legal aspects of what will happen to my shares of the Flint mill, should I happen to die after I am married.'

Robert held up a staying hand. 'No need for that, it's obvious. Your shares will go to your husband. It is, after all, the law, and we all know whose side the law is on. The side of the aristocracy, naturally.'

'Not necessarily,' put in Standish quietly.

Trying to hide her distaste for her

cousin, Patricia leaned forward. 'Lord Percy and I have spoken. He is of no mind to add the shares of the Flint mill to his assets. He recognises that the Flint family — your father and mine — built up the business, and that it is my wish that eventually you and your heirs should inherit them. Any children that result from my marriage will be well provided for. The Flint mill should remain in Flint ownership.'

Eyes narrowing, Robert looked at her with suspicion. 'And why would Lord Alexander do that?'

'Because,' said Patricia, 'it is part of our contract. His and mine.' She looked at him levelly. 'This marriage is almost a business matter.'

John Standish coughed. Patricia ignored him. 'The profits from the sale of the Pickering mill are mine, and they will form part of the Wakefield Hall estate as soon as I marry, along with the rest of my possessions. I will, however, have a large say in the way the money is to be used.'

Robert tossed off a snort of derision. 'And you believe that?'

'Of course I do.'

'Well, I never had you down to be so bird-witted.'

'Well,' retorted Patricia, 'I never had you down to be so mean-spirited either. I need not have set up this meeting, Robert, and might I remind you, the documents pertaining to the Flint mill shares are not yet signed!'

Indolently, Robert tipped his chair back and scowled. 'You can sign whatever papers you like, you and Standish between you. You think I don't know that they're worthless? Some smooth-talking lawyer employed by Lord Alexander would soon weasel all relevance out of it and I would be left exactly as planned — with nothing. You act out this . . . this *charade*, merely to appease my sensibilities.'

Patricia had seldom felt so angry; she felt her face go white. 'No, I do not,' she said. 'For you have none. I truly think, Robert, you were born with no feelings at all. I should have thought you'd be happy at my good fortune, and grateful that I want to make the mill shares safe for your family, should you have one, in the future. But no — you whine on like a veritable old woman about what you *should have*, never thinking to work for it.'

For a moment she scrutinised him as he lounged in his chair, resembling nothing so much as a study in arrogant indolence, and her grey eyes smouldered. 'You're quite capable of running that mill efficiently and profitably, yet you are milking the profits, not investing in new machinery. You are frittering money away, losing at the races, and loitering at the theatre. You're living an easy life and not looking to the consequences.

'Let me tell you, Robert, the only reason I'm taking such pains that the shares stay with the Flint line is because my father desired it. He also trusted me to oversee all your major decisions, which is why I was left a half share in the first instance.' Her sudden anger left her and she stopped speaking for a moment and gave a sigh. 'Now, you are not stupid, and you know all this to be true. Accept with good grace that you own only half of the mill. Improve your management of it, as I know perfectly well that you can, and perhaps in time to come, we'll talk further.'

'That will never come to pass,' said Robert through tightly compressed lips. 'Lord Alexander will never allow it.'

He quailed before the steely glance Patricia bestowed upon him. 'We'll leave Lord Alexander's name out of this, I think,' she said quietly.

Sullenly and silently Robert watched the papers being drawn up, but Patricia could sense the burning resentment he was trying hard to supress. Occasionally he threw a petulant glance towards the solicitor, John Standish, who had been noticeably quiet throughout the entire interview.

'Now, I think that's all for the present,' declared Patricia. 'You are still very welcome at my wedding, Robert. In fact it would be quite remarkable if you did not attend, would it not? And we shouldn't like to cause remark in the neighbourhood.'

Robert rose to his feet. 'Oh, I daresay you consider yourself very clever, but I shall get my own back — you see if I don't.'

He looked at her one last time before swinging himself out of the office without even a glance in the direction of John Standish.

'Good,' said Patricia, trying to mask the fact that the intensity of Robert's bitterness had caught her off guard for a moment. 'At least that's over with. It's a pity my uncle died so young and therefore had little to do with the mill.

'But my father gave Robert every opportunity — he just couldn't be bothered. Unfortunately his mother spoilt him . . . When he's had time to think, he'll understand that what I'm doing is not only carrying out my father's wishes but is also in his best interests.'

She looked across at John Standish, who was regarding her with respect tempered with some trepidation. Impatiently she shrugged her shoulders. 'Oh, very well, I admit my temper got a little out of hand, but truly, there seems there is nothing I can do to please him. He's just a spoilt child. His threats mean nothing.'

'I trust you are right,' answered John Standish gravely.

* * *

Nevertheless, over the next few days, Patricia did begin to regret the hastiness of her words to Robert. She knew full well that in the throes of growing up, she'd had a quick temper born mainly from the frustration of living in a man's world where it seemed impossible to express an opinion without being labelled overbearing and bossy.

Until now, she had thought her unruly temper to be a fault she'd left behind in her girlhood. She supposed it must have been the sight of her cousin sulkily lolling back in his seat like a truculent five-year-old denied a new toy that had sparked off her outburst. Perhaps, also, his thinly-veiled insinuation that she was marrying out of her class for prestige and profit only — which she reminded herself, was surely true — had caught her on the raw.

Somehow having the bare facts driven home had made her feel uncomfortable. She thought long and hard about her father. What would he advise her to do?

Eventually she made up her mind. Because they both used the same livery stable, she knew full well the days that Robert chose to go riding. Since meeting up with him accidentally on several occasions, she'd made it her business to choose an earlier time of the clock on those days to visit the stables herself, but this morning she deliberately arrived at a time when she thought he would be there.

In an offhand manner she enquired as to whether her cousin had been in yet today, to be told that he was expected shortly. She whiled away another twenty minutes in conversation before mounting Firefly, her usual chestnut mare which had been made ready, and had just about given up all hope of catching him that day when he strode into the yard.

She smiled cordially. 'Good morning, Robert.'

Robert halted and stood as though carved from stone, then slowly allowed his eyes to travel up over the handsome chestnut mare and her own tensely held body, finally let them come to rest upon her face. The sheer malevolence in his gaze made her draw in her breath.

For a moment it was touch and go whether he cut her acquaintance completely, but suddenly he gave a curt nod in her direction and called to have his horse brought.

'Do you ride alone this morning,

cousin?' Patricia enquired in a low voice. 'I can't quite like us to be bad friends and am come to apologise for my bad humour the last time we met.'

'Indeed?' returned Robert coolly. 'Well, I'm riding out of town on the Dewsbury country road and cannot prevent you from accompanying me — if you wish to do so.'

Undecidedly Patricia looked down at the top of his hat and his square-cut shoulders. He wasn't looking in her direction. Was this an acceptance of her olive branch or just a show of politeness for the sake of form?

'Well then, I shall go on ahead. Perhaps you'll catch me up, Robert, before we reach the turnpike.'

Another nod.

Patricia turned the chestnut and clattered out of the yard.

The sun was climbing high in the sky as she took the west road that led to Dewsbury. The country road was dry for lack of rain, and dust lay on the roadside brambles. She rode slowly, only half her attention on the road. The remainder was occupied with how she would find Percy's siblings, Percy's household — Percy's whole life, in fact, for the date of the wedding loomed.

'Bit of a circus, I expect,' Percy had said about their forthcoming nuptials. 'Still, nothing for it — got to be done. Best you don't see too much of Wakefield Hall beforehand, best you're introduced as Lady Percy Alexander — then that's how you'll always be thought of. Best start as you mean to go on. Be respected then. Should warn you, though, Mrs Rivers, the house-keeper — she's a dragon; advisable to get her on your side immediately. Don't stand any nonsense, mind. Worshipped my father, you know. Well, they all did. Afraid I'm a poor substitute.'

'You're not. I won't let you say so,' said Patricia hotly. 'Of course not. Different times . . . ' she broke off suddenly aware that she was starting to sound like Percy. 'I mean,' she went on hurriedly. 'You're a different master, bound to be so. You could very well be even better — and I'm sure they love you just as much.'

Percy gave her his usual sudden wide smile. 'Think so, Patricia? Well, that's good news, eh?' He frowned suddenly. 'No doubt about it, the place could do with a clean-up ... Needs a woman's touch. Not sure Mrs Rivers is a woman, for all she wears a skirt. Wouldn't like to take a wager on it. More like a sergeant major — eh?'

Thinking of this conversation now, Patricia smiled. Percy was just so ridiculous, so very approachable, not at all as she'd thought a lord would be.

Then her smile faded as she heard the steady clip clop of hooves behind her. She turned her head. Sure enough, Robert was catching her up. She hoped he'd left his sulks on the road behind him.

As he drew level with her, she glanced at him warily. He had his horse fall into step beside her.

She drew a slow intake of breath. 'I

always had a pesky temper, Robert, and I'm sorry for it. My nerves are a little on edge with the wedding arrangements and all.'

Robert still didn't look at her.

Patricia bit her lip. 'Well, I have said sorry. You must know that I shan't grovel before you.'

He gave a small laugh. 'Oh yes,' he said. 'I know that full well. But I daresay I'm at fault too. We are too much alike, you and I . . . We both like to have our own way. But I take my hat off to you, Pat. You played a good hand. It seems you're set up for life and will hold a powerful position in society. Good luck to you.'

'Thank you, Robert,' murmured Patricia, unsure whether she appreciated being likened to her cousin.

He gave her a sidelong glance. 'How say you we get off this road and go for a canter before we reach the turnpike?'

'What an excellent idea,' replied Patricia.

They cantered together across ground

that was hard for lack of rainfall. The streams still ran, but not as fiercely as was usual at this time of year.

'We need rain,' observed Robert as they slowed down again to walking pace. He dismounted and let his horse munch at the grass. Patricia followed his lead, slipping from the saddle and leaning at the chestnut's side.

'Nice little mare,' commented Robert, observing her. He put his hand in his pocket and pulled out a couple of sugar lumps.

Patricia watched as he fed one to his own horse and the other to hers. Perhaps she'd been wrong about him. A man who carried sugar lumps for his horses could surely not be all bad!

She carried on watching, shielding her eyes against the sun, as her cousin inspected the chestnut, patting her rump, feeling her legs and her withers before stroking her nose. 'Yes, nice little mare,' he repeated once again, handing the reins back to Patricia.

Not talking much, they led their

horses for a while.

'I suppose it's time I looked for a wife,' said Robert suddenly.

'If you've a mind to,' agreed Patricia thinking that in fact, yes, family responsibilities would be a good thing for Robert.

'I wasted the last year or so waiting for you didn't I?'

Oh no, not again.

'Come on, let's ride again.' Patricia put her boot in the stirrup and pulled herself into the saddle. The chestnut danced a little skittishly.

'No more sugar for you,' she admonished. 'I'll head back now Robert,' she called in his general direction.

'Right. I'm off to continue my ride. I've a mind to go up to the moors.'

Trying to quieten her horse, Patricia screwed her eyes against the sun and watched as Robert galloped off stylishly across the grass. She gave a grin. Still showing off — how typical. Expecting him to look back and wave she remained stationary for a moment, but he didn't so much as glance over his shoulder before disappearing out of sight.

Oh well — at least they were speaking again.

Humming softly to herself she turned the chestnut and set her to canter back to the road. But something was wrong. The chestnut snorted and reared on her back legs.

Somehow Patricia held her seat.

'Whoa now, girl! Gently does it.' Patricia eased herself out of the saddle. 'We'll walk then, for a little — if you're in a pesky mood.'

Although it took much longer than she would have liked, she led the horse gently over the meadow land and back to the field near the west road.

'Easy now, girl, I'm going to ride again now. If you've any objections, landing on the field will be softer for me than the road.'

Her side saddle moved downwards as she swung her weight into it. Firefly stood still obligingly.

'Good girl!' She sat back and

tentatively walked the chestnut forward.

But Firefly, it seemed, had other ideas. They had hardly gone three paces before her ears flattened and she bucked and snorted.

Patricia didn't even have time to scream; she felt herself falling. Then everything went black.

7

It seemed to Lord Percy Alexander that he simply hadn't had enough hours in the day recently. There had been so much estate business, so many people to see, lawyers to consult and other matters of a trivial yet personal nature that he felt he'd seriously neglected his fiancée. This was not a state of affairs which he relished. He felt he should be spending far more time with her. Time in reassuring her, slowly easing her into the idea of her new role — which, although he had every confidence she would fulfil quite adequately, he knew must appear a little daunting to someone not born to it.

This afternoon, therefore, he intended to put this state of affairs to rights. His plan was to call on the lady and persuade her to join him on a leisurely drive, perhaps taking in the home farm and introducing her to the farm manager and his new young wife, with whom he felt that Patricia could easily form a friendship.

He also planned to maybe wander off the country roads a little, spread a blanket in the meadow by the brook and indulge in a little courtship. The notion had occurred that she might not be too averse to a chance of repeating some of the kisses they had exchanged, and maybe exploring the possibilities in further depth. He remembered the unexpected sweetness of their first kiss; recalled the startled depths to her smoky eyes, which revealed an altogether unsuspected passion in her soul. She'd seemed as surprised and perplexed by the effect of his kiss as he had been relieved and amused. Altogether Percy found he was rather impatient to progress the wooing of his fiancée.

The weather was good; had been so for some time. Noticing that the streams were lower than usual and the ditches were all but dried up, he was almost on the verge of wishing for more rain. Not today, though; tomorrow would be much more convenient.

The open-topped carriage bowled along the dry country road between Dewsbury and Wakefield. The heavens were of a blue comparable to Mediterranean skies, but without the searing heat to accompany them. Percy surveyed the grassland to the side of him. Despite the lack of rain, it still looked lush and healthy. It was an idyllic scene.

There was a lone mare, a chestnut, cropping idly at the grass. As he watched, she glanced anxiously over her shoulder and shook at her saddle. He looked more closely. Where was her rider?

Percy stared as the mare turned her head again and nuzzled at what appeared to be a heap of blue cloth on the grass near to where she was grazing. He remembered that Patricia rode a chestnut mare.

A hideous fear began to make itself felt in the region of his breast bone.

'Whoa there!' Luckily he was on an open stretch of road. He pulled his horses up and tied the reins to an overhanging branch.

He peered over the hawthorn hedge. The heap of blue material took on a feminine form. It lay very still.

Somehow he managed to push through the hedge at a place where it naturally thinned. On legs that had unaccountably become weak, he moved closer to the horse and its would-be rider. His heart was hammering hard in his chest and there was a sick feeling in his stomach.

My God! It is her!

'Patricia,' he gasped, falling to his knees in front of her prone form. 'Pat, can you hear me? It's Percy.'

He looked down at her pale face with its well-marked eyebrows, neat nose, full, sweet lips and determined chin. Was she still breathing?

He put his fingers to her throat and felt a faint pulse. Her bluish-white eyelids fluttered open as he watched and she struggled to sit up.

'Oh, dear Lord . . . It seems I've taken a tumble.' She put a hand to her head. 'How careless, how very stupid.'

The overwhelming relief that swept over Percy threatened to turn him into a sobbing child again.

She seemed to half register his presence. 'Oh, it's you . . . Oh dear, please excuse me. I think, I think I might be sick.'

He gave a smile that wobbled a little and gently lowered her back into a lying position. 'Keep very still Patricia, very still. You've had a shock.'

She looked for a moment as though she might argue then, with a sigh, relaxed back and half-closed her eyes. For a few moments Percy sat quietly next to her, stroking her hand — although whether in order to reassure her or himself, he wasn't certain.

'Where does it hurt?' he asked when he was able.

'Everywhere,' said Patricia faintly. 'I no longer think I will cast up my accounts, but my head is swimming and I feel cold.'

'Blanket in the carriage,' Percy said immediately. 'You're shivering. Must be the shock. Hold on, Patricia, I'll fetch it.'

A few moments later and the blanket was tucked round her. Nothing was broken, she insisted, trying to smile; she could move everything as far as she could tell, but her head was still thumping and it just served her right for being so careless as to fall from her horse.

'I'd feel better sitting up, Percy, if it's not asking too much.'

'Be quiet, Patricia — doing it a shade too brown here. You're being very brave — no need to overdo it. Get you sitting up in a trice.' He looked round. 'Right, lie still and close your eyes for just a minute longer.'

'Yes, Percy,' murmured Patricia with a docility that was worryingly uncharacteristic of her.

Percy caught the chestnut by the

reins. 'What happened here, girl?' he asked softly. The chestnut put her head down looking slightly ashamed.

'Have to get you a decent horse,' he called over his shoulder. 'Can't have this kind of fandango.' He bent his head in an effort to remove the saddle. 'I'll put the saddle up against the hedge and you can lean against it until you feel well enough to stand.'

The chestnut's ears flattened and she bucked away from him. 'Easy, girl,' Percy soothed the animal before lifting the heavy saddle from her back. His eyes narrowed. 'Hey ho, what have we here?' He lifted a sprig of hawthorn from where it was wedged between the saddle and the chestnut's back.

'How on earth — ?' he began. Then he glanced back over his shoulder at Patricia, noticing again how pale she was.

Grim-faced, he put the hawthorn to one side, took the saddle and settled it against the hedge.

'When you're feeling more the thing,

you can put your arm round my neck and I'll carry you to the gate. Then you can rest a little before I help you into my carriage.'

'I'm sure I can walk, Percy. I'm perfectly fine, really.'

Patricia struggled to sit up and lift herself from the ground, whereupon it immediately became apparent that she wasn't fine at all. With a little cry of weakness she fell back.

'Told you so,' said Percy pragmatically. 'Now we'll do it my way.'

'You're exceedingly bossy,' Patricia answered faintly. 'But I'm so very glad you found me Percy. So very, very, glad.'

★ ★ ★

It was quite some time later that Percy deposited Patricia back at her home in Wakefield. Brooke the butler dispatched a footman to fetch a doctor and Percy sat nervously in the hall while his fiancée was examined, before eventually being pronounced fit but needing complete rest for a day or so.

Once the doctor had left, Percy stood by Patricia's bedside. She was obviously groggy from the sleeping draught given her by the doctor.

She opened one eye and smiled at Percy. 'Thank you,' she murmured. 'Don't know how I'd have managed. Robert had gone on — was going to ride on the moors, wouldn't have come back the same way. I might never have been found at all.'

'Robert?' Percy's expression of concern turned stony. 'I thought, since he was so oafish when you told him your plans for the mill, you were no longer on speaking terms — though what he had to be oafish about, I don't know. Consider you've been very generous . . . How come Robert was there?'

Patricia sighed. 'I wanted to make amends so I apologised for being so provoking on that occasion — because I was, you know. I can be quite — quite waspish with my tongue. Anyway I deliberately went to the stables when I knew he'd likely put in an appearance.' She paused in order to gather her strength. 'Of course, at first he was quite starched-up, you know, but then, well, he caught me up and we rode along together and chatted quite easily, even had a canter . . . ' For a moment puzzlement flickered in her eyes. 'Firefly was beautifully behaved then, I really don't understand . . . '

Percy squeezed her hand. 'Then what happened?'

It seemed an effort for her to remember and a frown appeared between her eyebrows. 'Oh, we talked on for a bit, he wished me well and he said what a good little mare Firefly was. He looked her over, the way men do. He knows quite a lot about horses, actually . . . '

'Indeed?' said Percy shortly.

'Then I said I was going to head back home because, actually, I hoped you might call today and I didn't want to miss you.'

He gave a curt nod. 'So did he help you into the saddle?'

Her heavy eyelids drooped and closed.

After staring for a moment, wondering exactly when it was that this face, this woman, had come to make him feel so fierce on her behalf, Percy turned away, thinking to let her sleep.

Then her eyes flickered open again. 'No, he didn't. I think we both mounted at the same time,' she went on, her voice thick with the desire to sleep. 'But Firefly was no trouble for me to mount. She's a small horse and I'm quite able — I assure you . . . But once I was up she was skittish so I dismounted and walked her for a way. By that time, of course, Robert was long gone . . . When we were in sight of the road I thought I'd try her again. And, well — she threw me . . . You know the rest.' She gave a sudden wide yawn. 'Oh forgive me . . . I'm so very sleepy.'

'Sleep now, Patricia. Don't worry, you're quite safe.'

Patricia gave a smile. 'Of course I am,

Percy. You do talk nonsense, but you are very sweet.'

After kissing her forehead, wearing an expression that had she seen it, Patricia would have described as far from sweet, Percy went downstairs and had a short conversation with Brooke.

No one, he explained, other than the doctor or her maid was to be allowed to disturb his fiancée, until he himself called the next morning and on no account was Mr Robert Flint to be given access to the premises.

Then with an expression of stony determination on his face, Percy drove his carriage back to the field where the chestnut stood staring forlornly into the distance. He retrieved the wicked piece of hawthorn from the top of the gate post where he'd left it, tethered Firefly to the back of his carriage and led her back to the livery stable. Casually, he enquired as to whether Mr Robert Flint had returned back from his ride and was told that he had done — quite some time ago.

'He is in good health, I trust?' asked Percy with an edge to his voice.

'Believe so, my lord. In fact he was quite jovial,' answered the stable boy.

'Jovial, eh?' responded Percy. Then, as he climbed back into his carriage, he added, 'Have to see if we can alter that.'

'Yes, sir,' said the stable boy uncertainly.

Percy visited four different taverns before he found the one which Mr Robert Flint apparently frequented on a regular basis. He was told that if he cared to sit in the small private parlour and partake of some refreshment, the landlord would bring Mr Flint to wait on him as soon as he put in an appearance at the hostelry. Percy offered his thanks and sat down with a bottle of good claret and a piece of pie, to wait.

After some thirty minutes during which time he had enacted in his imagination, the tearing of each and every one of Robert's limbs from his body, the landlord appeared with Robert in tow.

'Much obliged,' said Lord Percy. 'No,

don't bring another glass. Mr Flint won't be staying.'

Eyeing Percy somewhat dubiously, a pale-faced Robert came forward into the room with an outstretched hand. 'Good evening, my lord.'

'Is it?' Percy ignored the hand.

Robert smiled uneasily. 'I believe so, sir . . . Unless, that is, you have anything untoward to tell me.'

Percy regarded Robert expressionlessly. 'Untoward? And what might you expect me to tell you that might be described as untoward — eh?'

'Um, I'm sure I don't know, sir.'

'Perhaps you'd like to hazard a guess? What? Oh, come on, Mr Flint, do. Intelligent young fellow like yourself . . . You must have some idea of what would be likely to happen if a young lady mounts a horse when a lethal piece of hawthorn has been wedged under the saddle?'

Robert had turned yet paler.

'Perhaps the young lady, your cousin for instance, would be thrown from the

saddle, her head dashed against a stone
. . . Could very well kill her. Perhaps
she'd be left lying there with a broken
back, or neck, until someone happened
past? What think you?'

Robert licked dry lips. 'What are you
telling me, my lord?'

Suddenly Percy grew tired of the game.

'Your cousin, Mrs Pickering, went to
great lengths to explain to me that her
shares in the Flint mill were to be kept
in the Flint family.' He paused. 'Your
heirs, you comprehend? She even, so I
hear, took pains to clarify this with you
prior to our nuptials taking place.
Considerate of her, I thought.'

Robert said nothing, biting his lip.

'Mrs Pickering is a lady of her word
and I gave her my word that her wishes
would be upheld.' He broke off and
levelled a look at Robert that might
have scorched his eyebrows, had he
been an inch nearer. 'You're a greedy
man, Mr Flint. It obviously occurred to
you that if Mrs Pickering were to meet
with an accident before her marriage

you, as her next of kin, would stand to inherit everything she owns.'

Robert was sheet-white. 'Wh- what has happened to my cousin?'

Percy took a turn about the room before answering.

'Always considered myself to be a mild-mannered sort of fellow,' he remarked eventually in a deceptively easy tone. 'Would like to keep it that way. But hear this.' He stopped in front of Robert and stared in a way that caused the other man to take a step back. 'Upset Mrs Pickering, you upset me — eh? Sure you take my meaning!'

Robert coloured and blustered. 'I'm sure I don't understand what you're insinuating, my lord. Patricia and I had words at the solicitor's, I own to that. Though why she'd take umbrage . . . I only meant to remind her of her duty.'

Abruptly, Lord Percy's expression changed. His eyes hardened to granite. He took a pace closer and seized a surprised-looking Robert by his lapels.

'Remind her of her duty?' he

repeated. 'Her duty — to you? You jest, sir. Mrs Pickering owes you nothing! Mrs Pickering is recovering from her fall. She doesn't know that you were instrumental in the fall, and she doesn't need to know, but if anything befalls Mrs Pickering at any time in the future, then I swear I will kill you with my own bare hands. Do you understand?'

'This is nothing but a Banbury tale,' Robert squeaked. 'My cousin was well when I left her. She will tell you so herself.'

Percy brought his face up close to his. 'You lie, sir, and you disgust me!'

Just as suddenly as he'd grasped them, he let go of Robert's lapels. Robert lost his balance and staggered against the wall.

'Good day to you, Mr Flint,' said Percy dismissively, dusting his hands off one against the other. 'You may go.'

He turned his back and made to sit down and finish his drink, only to feel a sudden rush of air and a violent push from behind.

Expelling a breath, he quickly wheeled round. There was a fast movement of his arm and fist, followed by a cracking sound.

Robert staggered back, clutching at his jaw.

Percy looked down at him sprawled on the floor.

'Devil take it . . . Didn't want it to come to this.' Calmly he took the piece of hawthorn from his breast pocket, bent down and closed Robert's fingers round it. 'Allow me to present you with a reminder of our talk.' He squeezed Robert's fingers more tightly. Robert yelped with pain. 'Now, keep away from your cousin, Mr Flint,' he said quietly. 'And keep away from me.'

The landlord's anxious face appeared around the door. 'Everything all right here, my lord?'

'Perfectly, I thank you. Mr Flint tripped, but he is leaving now.' Lord Percy gave a disarming smile. 'It's a fine claret you serve here — oh, and I'll have another piece of pie.'

8

Nervously, Patricia sat on the edge of the unfamiliar four-poster bed in the sumptuous bridal suit of the best hotel that Sheffield had to offer. Her eyes were huge in her face; her dark hair set free of its fastenings, massed over her shoulders in a cloud. After examining her anxious reflection in the glass and being scarce able to recognise herself, she had reluctantly dismissed her maid and now sat in her white embroidered nightgown awaiting Percy's arrival.

She found it slightly surprising that someone like herself, so very matter-of-fact and businesslike, should feel so tense and unsure. *It's only Percy, she told herself, and you're no silly miss; you know full well what to expect. Just lie still until it's over. Only try to be a good wife.*

In an effort to calm herself and stop

her foolish heart from beating so crazily, she breathed deeply and tried to think of the recent past rather than the immediate future.

But the day had moved so swiftly, she found that she could hardly remember the ceremony nor the celebration that followed.

Mr John Standish had given her away. Percy's brother, Johnny, had acted as his best man and his sister Katherine as her bridesmaid. Johnny had turned out to be a younger, darker version of Percy with an identical ready grin, and Katherine a sweetly pretty girl with light-coloured curls and the same warm brown eyes as her siblings. They'd had hardly time to do more than be introduced before the ceremony was upon them, but Patricia felt already as though they had accepted her as part of the family.

Despite the private wishes of the bride and groom for a small celebration, the wedding had been well-attended. After they'd exchanged their vows and turned to make their way back down the aisle, Patricia blinked her eyes in an effort to pick out individuals from the sea of pale moon faces and feathered hats that merged in front of her. For a moment she panicked. Surely it must be that she could discern a known, friendly face to represent her own acquaintances and family?

Then, of course, as the church interior swung back into focus, she realised that yes, there was a fair representation of her mother's side of the family as well as many friends of long standing — although somehow, it seemed, she'd managed to miss Robert at the ceremony.

Later, when the wedding breakfast was in progress, she'd combed the crowd again and was perturbed when, once more, the search proved to be fruitless. Her cousin was conspicuous by his absence.

Briefly, she recalled the strangely enigmatic conversation she'd had with Percy not long after her fall from Firefly. 'Does Robert know of my accident?'

she had asked him.

Percy examined his fingernails. 'Yes, he does,' he'd answered shortly.

'Oh . . . We parted on such good terms, I thought that he might have visited to see how I fared.'

'Did you want him to visit?'

'Yes. Well — I suppose no. Probably best not before the wedding, wouldn't you say?'

'Yes, I would say — best not!'

Patricia let her mind linger for a moment on the ride she'd taken with Robert that had immediately preceded her fall. She remembered the violently bucking horse. A frown appeared between her brows. 'It was uncharacteristic, Firefly behaving in that fashion.'

'Yes, indeed. Most peculiar. She must have been in a strange humour. Now, we agreed to discuss music for the wedding, did we not? Something jolly, I thought, to finish . . . '

So the moment had passed. But still from time to time Patricia found her thoughts returning to the strangeness of

Firefly's sudden, freakish behaviour and the silence of Robert.

Now, as she sat on the bed, considering whether she should actually get under the covers or not, she began to wonder about Percy's own demeanour. He had seemed distinctly odd in the remaining days between her accident and the wedding. It had crossed her mind on a few occasions to wonder whether he was regretting his decision to wed her; whether he thought, after all, that a marriage of convenience could not make up for the difference in their social status. Although, she conceded, he was not high in the instep with her in any way — it was just that he seemed distracted and slightly bothered about something.

In her worst moments she wondered if he wished he'd never met her.

There was a tap on the door.

Patricia drew in a breath but when she opened her mouth to form the words 'come in', no sound came out.

The door handle turned anyway and Percy, in an open-necked night shirt, strode into the room.

'Evening Lady Pat,' he said briskly. And then, taking in her slight form sitting on the edge of the bed, her hair loose and spread around her, he stopped. 'You look like a frightened child, Mrs Pickering — I mean, Lady Pat . . . Surely not scared of me, are you?'

'A little,' said Patricia between chattering teeth.

'No need to be,' said Percy gently. 'Promise you I won't do anything you won't like — eh?'

He pulled back the covers and got into bed, giving her a friendly smile. 'Care to join me?'

Patricia licked her dry lips. 'First — there's something I need, I want to say . . . I explained to you before that I didn't, that I couldn't always please my husband.' She moistened her lips again. 'I don't know why, quite, but if there is something amiss with me — if I fail to please you in any way . . . '

She risked a glance at Percy; his eyes

looked sympathetic but puzzled. 'Lordy, Lady Pat. Don't need to make such a business of it, you know. Ain't that difficult. Damned if you won't find you like it before the week's out.'

Despite her anxiety, Patricia found herself smiling. 'What I'm trying to say, Percy, is that I fully comprehend the ways of the gentry. I want a child, you want an heir, we both want this marriage to be a success but if we find we don't quite suit in this regard . . . ' She patted the bed. 'I will never object or be unreasonable if you wish to, want to, well — take a mistress.'

There — she'd said it. An enormous sense of relief threatened to overwhelm her.

Percy was also smiling; a perplexed smile rather as though to a non-comprehending child.

'Lord. Never knew a person to want to make things so plain. Now, come to bed Patricia and we'll see what we make of each other. May take you a while to get used to it . . . Some ladies never really get the hang of it, so they say. Still, dare say you will — seem a game sort of girl to me.'

Gingerly, Patricia got into bed and lay straight as a board, her arms by her sides. Percy leaned on one elbow looking down at her.

'Mrs Pickering, Patricia, Lady Pat, that is — d'you mind if I kiss you?'

He traced the side of her cheekbone with his finger and tilted her chin up towards him. 'Think you might like it. Think you did last time. Feels like a long time ago since then.' He gave a crooked smile. 'Sometimes I feel as though it never happened.'

Patricia turned her face towards his.

'Oh, Percy,' she whispered. 'So do I.'

Percy kissed her and Patricia felt herself spiralling towards a new feeling that was almost — yes, it was — pleasurable.

'There now, that wasn't so bad, was it?'

Patricia said nothing, waiting for what was to come next, which in her first marriage, had never been an agreeable experience. But she knew her duty, and she wanted a baby, didn't she?

She gritted her teeth.

★ ★ ★

Percy had arranged that they stay for two nights in Sheffield which, although built in the fine setting of an amphitheatre of south Pennine hills, in itself was a city of no great remark. Travelling on from there, they stayed in Leicester with its market square and medieval Guild Hall. The weather remained fine but not too hot, allowing them to take a pleasant stroll past the castle ruins and along the banks of the canal, which was extensively used by narrow boats taking goods from the Midlands to London.

From there they travelled on at a smarter pace, stopping only once more, this time in Hertfordshire, before heading off early in the morning towards London where the Alexander town house had been made ready for them.

It was a house of some magnificence in close proximity to Barclay Square. Percy was relieved to find that his memory had not proved him wrong and that, here at least, the standards of housekeeping had not slipped. The town house smelled of beeswax, lavender and fresh linen, and the sparking windows let in shafts of welcoming sunshine. Fairbrass was right; it would be a crying shame to sell such a house.

Knowing it might well still come to that, Percy gave a sigh. Then, watching his new wife's expression, the frown between his brows lifted and he gave himself over to enjoying showing the house to his new bride.

If Patricia was overawed by her surroundings, Percy was the only one who would have suspected it. He had wondered whether she would be intimidated by having so many servants to do her bidding, but found that she had a quiet air of command about her that his old retainers warmed to.

That she would be a little shy in the bedchamber he had half expected from her earlier confidences, but he was a patient man and they had plenty of time. Meanwhile he wooed her gently and carefully; sometimes doing no more than holding her, caressing her tenderly until he felt the stiffness and anxiety gradually leave her body. Eventually she would sleep and he would lie there next to her, wondering about her previous experience of marriage.

Just as he had hoped and believed, they found they had many things in common. They chose not to tarry too long in fusty museums, but lingered in leafy squares and parks talking of their native Yorkshire and their separate childhood experiences. Little time was spent at the card tables, for neither had a taste for gambling. They attended a few concerts, but not of a mournful nature; they had discovered with delight that their preferences were for lively tunes — music for dancing. Very aware that this honeymoon might have to last them for quite some time to come, Percy did his very best to entertain his bride and make her feel comfortable.

Once in London, there were of course many things to occupy them. A number of invitations swiftly arrived and Lord and Lady Alexander accepted requests for their company at various dinners, soirees, assemblies and balls. To his joy, Percy discovered that his new wife was more than competent on the dance floor. Somehow, after finding her so tense and reticent in the bedchamber, and recalling how very gradually he'd been obliged to coax her like a nervous young filly towards the marriage consummation, he'd thought that all things physical must be something of a trial to her. But from the moment he took her in his arms, she appeared relaxed and fitted her body elegantly alongside his. They swirled around the dance floor, Percy guiding her steps and feeling as though in a dream. Sometimes he felt he never wanted the waltz to finish, only noticing as the last notes of music died away that many a gentleman's quizzing glass was lifted in the direction of his wife's graceful figure. At first he was unsure whether to be amused or outraged by this. Eventually, he decided that actually it was a compliment of the highest order — and as long as Patricia was so obviously enjoying herself, he was happy too.

And then, of course, there were the shops.

'We must buy presents for your brother and sister while we're away,' Patricia prompted him.

'Presents, eh? Well — never would have thought of that.'

'It would be a good notion, would it not? I'd hate either of them to feel that my presence will in any way change things.'

'Change things? Of course it will change things; bound to. Change things for the better, I should say. Kitty — call her Kitty, y'know, dare say she'll want you to as well — she can't wait to have you live with us. She misses female company. Johnny won't mind too much, one way or the other. Mostly away. Cambridge. Female voice might be a good thing, though, keep him in check . . . Now, shopping. What d'you suggest?'

Wakefield shops, even the shops in York, had nothing to touch the variety of fripperies, fancies and fashions that London offered. Percy took her to the most exclusive stores and she responded with round-eyed wonder. It delighted him to see how openly shocked she was at his smallest intention to lavish money on her.

'Nonsense,' he said when she demurred at his extravagance. 'Can't be seen to be shabby with the purse strings. Next thing we'll know, tongues will be wagging that I'm all to let, and then the dunners will be hammering on the door. Anyway we're only staying for a se'nnight more. An economy in itself, wouldn't you say?'

'But Percy,' protested Patricia, laughing at his arguments, 'I need no more bonnets — truly I don't.'

'You do, mi'dear, now you're Lady

Percy Alexander. Besides, it suits you. Quite a beauty now I've tricked you out in the mode. Only funning about the creditors. Not in a state of utter penury yet, y'know.'

All in all Percy congratulated himself many times during his honeymoon on his brilliant notion of proposing to Patricia. He delighted in introducing her to his friends, confiding to them behind her back that it was a case of love at first sight — which, oddly enough, not one of them challenged.

Naturally, they would recall that he had been down earlier in the season in an unsuccessful attempt to find a bride, so why should they be surprised that he'd eventually found a love match on his very doorstep?

If any of them lifted an eyebrow in private, that she did not come from society's top drawer, they did not comment in public. Any bride who was chosen by Lord Alexander, it appeared, would be accepted without murmur.

Although Patricia had previously

stayed in the metropolis when attending the ladies' academy some years ago, the sights and sounds she was experiencing in Percy's company were very different and much more exciting. Her enjoyment of all London had to offer showed on her animated face, and Percy revelled in her happiness. She was gratifyingly impressed and enthralled with all of the entertainments and places Percy took her to.

Occasionally, he caught her watching him with a smile on her face that quite made him want to kiss her right then and there, in the middle of the street they were walking down or the concert they were attending — or, in fact, wherever they were situated. And she laughed a lot, too. Not a silly simpering giggle. More of a chuckle or a genuine full-throated laugh of amusement, which made him feel for a moment as though he was perhaps the wittiest man on earth. He found himself to be sporting what felt like an almost permanent idiotic grin.

Even when they were quiet together, sitting at dinner or walking in the park with her hand tucked into his arm, he felt a glow of wellbeing which he didn't quite understand, but still felt grateful for.

On their last day in London, they strolled around the park talking about nothing in particular and laughing just for laughing's sake.

Percy suddenly stopped. 'Well, Lady Pat,' he said fondly, staring at her very intently and thinking that her eyes, neither blue nor grey as they were, were actually just about the most taking pair of eyes he'd ever seen. 'Well, Lady Pat, how does being Lady Pat suit you?'

Patricia looked up at him. 'I believe, Lord Percy, that it suits me very well. Very well indeed!'

9

Patricia smoothed down the already smooth front of her gown and hugged her secret hope close to her. It was evening, and a golden light suffused the terrace and overgrown gardens beyond. They had taken a leisurely stroll around the sadly neglected knot garden, discussing how they would like it planted, with low lavender and box hedging, ready for next summer. Now Percy was having a quick word with Fairbrass and Johnny about tomorrow's proposed trip to York and when he had finished, they would go up to bed.

Suddenly aware that she found the thought heart-warming rather than slightly disconcerting she gave a quiet smile, realising that — after two months — she must be getting used to married life.

It was the end of August now. The harvest had been gathered in and her honeymoon was well and truly over. The house and its shabby magnificence no longer intimidated her, although she knew it would take longer for her to become used to the many staff that were part of the fabric of life in such a huge household.

She had expected to feel some trepidation, for she was very sure that all the staff at Wakefield Hall had her down as an upstart, nothing but a mill owner's daughter and not nearly good enough to so much as polish Lord Alexander's boots; but she also knew they'd have to hide their feelings — in Percy's presence, at least. And after all, she still had Trimble, her maid, and Brooke, her butler, to whom Percy had given the position of extra head footman — 'for we'll need extra staff now, Lady Pat,' he'd said.

Actually, until she'd seen them en masse standing at the great front entrance, she hadn't really found the thought of hostile servants so disconcerting. She reasoned that they surely couldn't be as bad as a room full of mill girls angry that their time was being reduced, and therefore, they thought — incorrectly, as it happened — their wages.

Well, she'd dealt with that little situation quite easily. She'd simply explained that the new machines would make the work faster, and more productive, so there would be fewer hours for them to work — but that, provided they worked just as hard, their wages would remain the same.

Anyway, her thoughts ran, compared to the ordeal of the marriage bed, coping with the servants was surely a minor matter.

Leading up to the wedding, the ordeal of 'the marriage bed' had loomed so great in Patricia's mind that she'd scarcely thought of anything else. Her first marriage had made her think she had no great taste or aptitude for the marriage act. She had done her duty, of course she had, but even though she had been as fond of Felix as though he were a brother, his visits to her bedchamber had been infrequent, the whole experience usually painful but mercifully quickly over with, and the subject was never, ever referred to by either of them in the cold light of day.

Even having discovered that Percy's kisses were acceptable, somewhat longer in duration than those of Felix and infinitely more pleasurable, she still expected that the same would be the case with Percy.

The one thing, or rather person, she hadn't built into the equation was Percy. Percy with his gentle ways, staccato speech and ready smile; Percy, who was sweet and kind, calm and tender. Oh yes, somehow she'd forgotten that Percy was just, well — Percy.

And she'd failed to recall the strange magic that seemed to descend as though from above every time he was close to her, the way her heart suddenly pounded for no good reason just at the touch of his hand on her wrist. In her anxiety, she'd forgotten all sorts of things.

Strange, then, that when it came to it — the moment she'd been dreading — there was no embarrassment. Percy just refused to be embarrassed; there was no fumbling or awkwardness, no sudden pain or soreness. They'd even laughed, for goodness' sake — and by the end of the honeymoon, Patricia was so intent on pleasing him that she forgot to think of herself at all, and she found she was enjoying the kisses, at least, more and more. So maybe it was possible after all to get used to it, this so-important part of married life.

But, as she was to discover, life at Wakefield Hall was not the same as a honeymoon in London. For a start there were always so many others around, and both she and Percy were continually busy. He with estate business and financial affairs; she with making friends of his siblings, entertaining local dignitaries to afternoon tea, and coping with household management. For Wakefield Hall was in dire

158

need of household management.

Mrs Rivers proved to be a tall lady who habitually dressed in clothes of unrelieved black. Added to the fact that she had the bearing of a sergeant major and a voice like iron filings, her face put Patricia in mind of a steel trap. The new Lady Alexander was wary but not completely defeated, for she quickly discovered the chink in Mrs Rivers armour. The chink was Kitty.

Unfortunately, on meeting her sister-in-law, Kitty had developed an immediate attachment — something which in any other circumstances Patricia would have considered a welcome blessing. Just now, however, every attention Kitty bestowed upon her was watched jealously by the key-carrying housekeeper.

With Percy's words echoing in her mind, Patricia decided she must start as she meant to go on. So, ignoring the stony expression of Mrs Rivers, she set about giving Wakefield Hall a much-needed, thorough going-over. Carpets were beaten, along with bed hangings and curtains. Chandeliers were lowered and cleaned, silver was polished with salt and vinegar, and the oak balustrades were soon gleaming with beeswax polish.

Mrs Rivers sniffed with clear umbrage whenever Patricia came near her and before the week was out, she felt compelled to confront the situation.

'I appreciate, Mrs Rivers,' she began, 'that you have had much to do in caring for a predominantly male household for so very long, and it must have been tedious to have your efforts go unrecognised. In my experience, men often seem oblivious to their surroundings and how very hard one has to work in order to achieve a high standard, but I hope you'll find that now Wakefield Hall has a new mistress, your efforts will not go unnoticed or commented upon.'

She paused, just long enough to catch Mrs Rivers' affronted eye, and gave a wide smile. 'And of course Kitty is growing up now, and is also becoming sensitive to the ambience of a house and the skill of its management. I'm sure that together, the three of us will very soon see a marked improvement.'

The housekeeper's expression had remained impassive and Patricia, knowing the war was not yet won, turned away.

It seemed the other servants, however, even though they might have had reservations at first, were warming to her calm, fair manner.

Percy's brother Johnny was usually out and about on the estate fishing and riding, or joining in occasional forays with friends to whatever delights the neighbouring towns had to offer. But he grinned whenever he saw her and took the time to say, 'Capital morning — eh?' in a way most reminiscent of Percy's endearing manner.

It was a busy life led in beautiful surroundings, and if only Patricia had been able to see more of Percy, she would have been happy. As it was, she sometimes felt she had dreamed the honeymoon period when she had been the centre of her husband's attention and their lives full of laughter.

But they were still close, she told herself. She had been surprised at first that although Percy had his own bedchamber, he consistently came to her bed to sleep. Well, not only to sleep, of course.

When she'd ventured the opinion, with a giggle, that it seemed like a waste of a room, Percy had stared at her. 'The separate rooms are only for form's sake,' he said. 'But if you'd rather not, Lady Pat — only have to say, y'know. My parents always shared a room. Seems a friendly thing to do, to me, but daresay not everyone agrees, eh?'

'Oh no, Percy. I like you sharing my room, don't misunderstand me ... ' She broke off in confusion.

'Hmm. Like it, do you? Thought you might, eventually.'

He yawned hugely, swung his legs into bed, curled himself round her and was asleep within minutes.

Recalling this now as Percy came

across the terrace through the warm evening air towards her, Patricia smiled.

'That's settled then,' her husband announced. 'Going to York tomorrow. Fairbrass stays here, so any problems, he's your man. Taking Johnny with me. Feel the need to make him aware of estate matters, a situation I never benefited from. Needs to meet men in wigs and know just where his living comes from in order to appreciate it — don't you think?'

Swallowing down disappointment that she was not to be included in the trip, Patricia nodded in agreement.

'York's beastly hot and smelly this time of year — you wouldn't enjoy it,' went on Percy as though reading her mind. 'Won't stay above a night or so — although Johnny will be bound to want to stay longer.'

Trying to ignore the sinking of her heart, Patricia took his arm as he led her in from the terrace and towards the staircase.

'Be back before you know it,' he said

squeezing her arm and nuzzling her hair just above her ear. 'Daresay you'll find plenty to do. The place looks neat as a pin already, though. You've made a home of it for us all, Pat — you've worked miracles.'

Like a cloak, a warm glow of happiness settled itself around her. Of course she could manage for two days without him; she'd find ways to keep herself busy.

The windows of their bedchamber were pushed wide open, and the sultry night air was full of the sounds of insects.

'Wonderful night indeed, Lady Pat!' He leaned towards her, his eyes full of humour but with a darkness to them that made Patricia's heart start hammering loudly in her ears. Suddenly, she found herself shuddering with anticipation.

He blew out the candle. 'Come, Lady Pat. Let's give ourselves something to remember over the next two days.'

* * *

Much later when, passion spent, Patricia found herself clinging to her husband with tears of surprised fulfilment in her eyes, she gazed up through the moonlight at his shadowy face.

'Oh, Percy,' she murmured in a voice that trembled. 'I never knew. I never knew it could be like this.'

Percy smiled against her hair.

'Didn't think so!' he said. 'Knew something not quite right with your first marriage, so had to proceed with caution.' He gave a wide smile and a low chuckle. 'Do know now, though, don't you — so that's all right, eh?'

She woke just after dawn to the sound of a blackbird's song. Percy was lying on his back, still snoring. She studied his profile. The strong nose, thick eyebrows and the smile lines that scored his cheeks. How had she ever thought he was only moderately attractive?

Then, as a sudden wave of nausea

overcame her, slowly so as not to disturb him, she slid out of bed. It was only early morning but she felt a sudden hunger for a dry biscuit perhaps, which she felt would combat the queasy feeling in her stomach.

A few minutes later, having only stopped to don her robe, she was making her way down the back stairs to the kitchen where she was sure someone would be able to find her some nourishment. She paused just outside the housekeeper's room at the sound of voices.

'Of course,' she heard Mrs Rivers saying, 'himself's off to York today where the mistress of his younger days resides. And we all know what that means, don't we?'

'No,' answered the voice of the cook sharply. 'Just keep your nasty suspicions to yourself. No need to think he's like his late lordship. Young Percy will be faithful — at least until he's got her with child.'

'Huh,' snorted Mrs Rivers. 'With his fancy piece living in York? He plans to

166

stay at least two nights — what does that tell you?'

Patricia didn't wait to hear the reply. Nausea forgotten, she turned and crept back up to her bed chamber.

Percy was still as she'd left him, but smiled in his sleep and draped an arm round her shaking shoulders as she slid back into bed.

She didn't sleep again. After turning herself to face away from him, she feigned sleep through his valet's discreet knock, through Percy's quiet instructions not to wake her yet, and intended to continue the charade until his early morning departure for York.

She had reckoned, however, without Percy.

An hour after he'd left her bedchamber, she heard him return and felt the depression of the mattress as he sat on the bed. She kept her eyes clamped tight shut.

'Lady Pat,' he murmured softly, stroking her cheek tenderly. 'I'm afraid I have to go now.'

Patricia opened her eyes. How foolish he must think she was, how naïve, to have lain trembling with pleasure in his arms last night, thinking he cared for her — thinking that what had just happened between them was special?

Suddenly she felt angry.

'Goodbye, Percy,' she said as though it couldn't matter less. 'Have a good time in York. Please feel free to do whatever you have a mind to.'

An expression of bewilderment passed over his brow. 'Not sure I perfectly understand you . . .'

'Oh, I am a woman of the world, Percy. I'm sure you understand me perfectly well. Let's not forget exactly what this marriage is about. You wanted money. You got it. I wanted a child. That was the bargain, was it not? And now you go to York.'

Percy stared at her for a long time, his expression of bafflement changing to one of slow comprehension. He leaned forward to take her face in his hands and made to kiss her lips.

Resolutely, Patricia turned her face away.

Instead, he kissed the side of her cheek. 'I'll not force you, Patricia. We'll speak further when I return.'

Patricia lay down, closed her eyes and said nothing. Only when she'd heard the clatter of his departing carriage on the cobbles below did she allow a tear to squeeze itself out from under her eyelids.

Mercifully she slept again, and on waking she was determined to pull herself together somehow. She needed to get away from the house; away from Mrs Rivers and her insidious tongue.

Sure enough, once she had breakfasted and ordered her carriage, she had talked herself into believing that of course she could learn to live with the fact that Percy had a mistress whom he would visit from time to time and that it was nothing short of downright greedy and ungrateful to expect otherwise from this marriage. Indeed how could she, when she'd been the one to intimate that she would find it acceptable for him to take a mistress?

That she hadn't considered that he might already have one of long-standing was beside the point.

Why then, as her carriage bowled along the country roads towards Wakefield, did she feel this sick, angry torment deep inside? It took her until she reached the Dewsbury road to put a name to this unpleasant new emotion she was experiencing.

It was jealousy.

Determined to stifle this bitter reaction which was so foreign to her nature, she looked about her. She slowed the horses as her carriage drew close to the place where she had been thrown by Firefly. Briefly she wondered what was at the bottom of her cousin's puzzling silence, and why Percy had been strangely reluctant to discuss her cousin since the wedding.

She looked up past the field, to where Robert and she had taken their canter together — and as though on cue, a rider appeared on the brow of the hill. Sure enough, as he advanced across the meadowland towards her, Patricia was able to make out his features and to establish that it was indeed her estranged cousin.

His expression as he approached was dour; indeed it crossed her mind that had he had access to the road in any other area, he would have chosen it and ignored her completely. As it was, he passed through the gate and drew his horse up alongside her on the road.

He gave her a surly, sidelong glance.

Unsmilingly, Patricia looked back.

'So, where's your fine husband this morning?' he asked in heavily sarcastic tones.

For a moment, Patricia wondered if the whole world had gone mad. Why wasn't Robert smiling, or at least explaining why he hadn't come to her wedding and why there had been this silence between them for so long?

'My husband,' she said at last, 'has gone to York. Not that it can in any way signify with you. I wonder that you are able to look me in the face . . . '

She broke off. She had been going to take him to task for not even having the manners to explain his absence from her wedding. After all, they'd parted friends, had they not, the last time they'd met? But suddenly she felt tired; felt bored with trying to read Robert's mind.

'Ah, so he told you then of our fall-out? It hardly surprises me. I never thought him to be a man of his word . . . So? Now I suppose he's off to York. Back to the bed of his mistress. Well, that's only to be expected — if you marry into the gentry.'

A cold feeling spread over Patricia. Was she the only one in the whole of Yorkshire not to be aware of Lord Alexander's mistress in York? Her mind shied away from that fact and homed in on the earlier part of his dialogue.

'What do you mean, Robert? Told me what? I never knew that you had ever met. What fall-out?'

Robert looked away with a shrug of disbelief. 'Don't pretend . . . He told you of our falling-out, of his ridiculous accusations, of him having forbidden me to come to the wedding, or to ever attempt to see you again?'

Then as Patricia still looked dumbfounded he went on petulantly, 'What? Did he tell you none of these things? Of how he accused me of setting a briar beneath your mare's saddle; of planning to kill you? Of his dastardly assault upon my person?'

'What?' demanded Patricia, her mind reeling.

But Robert was urging his horse forward.

'I'll wish you good day, cousin,' he said with a curl to his lip. He gave a sneering laugh. 'And I wish you good luck in your marriage — for all the good it will ever do you.'

A devastated Patricia was left staring after him.

10

Percy's business had been completed in two days and now he was anxious to return home. He had been correct when he'd told Patricia that York would be hot and horribly pungent at this time of year, it was why most citizens of refined sensibilities stayed away.

But the distasteful atmosphere of the city was not the only reason Percy was in a hurry to return to Wakefield Hall. His overriding motivation was the look in his new wife's eyes as she'd wished him goodbye. Somehow he hadn't been able to shift the feeling that something had suddenly gone very, very wrong.

Between her sinking into a deeply satisfied sleep and his waking the following morning, something had happened to hurt her and to make her distrust him. There weren't too many things that could be the cause of this, as

Percy knew full well. But he'd glimpsed the wounded expression in her eyes as she'd finally managed to form her lips round the word 'York', so he surmised it had to have something to do with York and his choosing to journey there without her.

Percy's lips tightened. She must have heard some tittle-tattle regarding his ex-mistress, it was the only explanation he could think of. Somehow he'd deemed it wiser not to mention the existence of his former mistress to Patricia. After all, the affair was well and truly over, and had been since his father's death. And he had seen too much distress caused by his father's constant infidelity to ever inflict the same thing on a wife of his own.

But surely that didn't mean he had to explain all this to Patricia? Surely she should know that he had probably had a mistress in the past, but that now he was a married man all that was behind him. He'd thought her to be a woman of the world and, for heaven's sake, she'd almost suggested herself that he might take a mistress, hadn't she? He racked his brains. And what had he said? Had he reassured her that it wouldn't be the case? Or had he just ignored the topic completely? Anyway, why would she suddenly start thinking about mistresses now?

Just as he felt they'd made a breakthrough, too. Just when Patricia had relaxed enough to recognise that the marriage act could be a wonderful thing — not just a trial to be borne in order to produce offspring. Of course, he'd always known her first marriage hadn't been a proper marriage. He'd somehow known that Patricia had a whole untapped well of passion inside her just waiting to be found. And bringing her to the point where she discovered it too, had been wonderful. He'd made her happy — he knew he had, and in so doing he'd made himself happy too. In fact he'd felt a tenderness he'd never experienced before. He'd felt protective and altogether as though he couldn't be more joyful if he was the king of England. Wonderful. Yes, that was it — wonderful.

But then morning had come, and for some reason the spell had been broken. Uncomprehendingly, Percy shook his head. There was no understanding the fairer sex.

He hoped he wouldn't have to start wooing her all over again. Although — he smiled — come to think of it, he'd thoroughly enjoyed the wooing of Mrs Pickering, or Lady Pat, as he loved to call her. It had almost been as though she'd never been married before — and he was the first . . .

'What are you smiling about?' asked Johnny who was sitting opposite him in the carriage. 'Although, suppose — don't need to ask really.'

'Eh?' said Percy jerking himself back to the present.

Johnny sported a grin from ear to ear. 'Mooning after Patricia again. You made a good choice, brother. If ever I get to be leg-shackled — not intending to, mind, till I'm at least thirty — if ever I did, though, I'd look around for someone like Pat. Capital girl. Capital!'

'Don't remember asking your opinion,' said Percy with a smile that belied the put-down. 'Glad you like her, though. Kitty likes her too . . . So do I,' he added as an afterthought.

Johnny gave a smirk. 'Noticed,' he said. 'Can't take your eyes off her whenever she's in the room . . . Smile all the time. Soppy smiles like just now. Tell when you're thinking about her . . . Obvious.'

'Is it?' said Percy in surprise. 'Well — yes. Pat makes me happy, I suppose, that's all.'

'Happy?' echoed Johnny incredulously. 'You're strutting around like a dog with two tails.'

'Have a care, brother. Just because I've taken you to York and treated you as an equal adult doesn't give you leave to ignore all delicacy, and take it upon yourself to lecture me in the ways of matrimony.'

'Wouldn't dream of it,' replied Johnny,

quite unabashed. 'Not while you're making such a cake of yourself all on your own.'

'Talking of making a cake of yourself, tell me how much blunt did you put up for that appalling waistcoat?'

Looking proudly down at the highly decorated yellow garment, Johnny grinned. 'Ain't that bad. Got to keep up with the mode. Not that you'd know too much about that . . . ' He looked pointedly at Percy's country attire.

Percy looked out of the window. 'Can't this dammed carriage go any faster?' he said, suddenly even more impatient to be home.

'Calm down, brother. She'll still be there, still be waiting for you.'

★ ★ ★

Johnny was right. Patricia was waiting for him. She was pacing the carpet, her mind a frenzy of what she would say and what she most definitely wouldn't say. Whether she would demand immediately to know what exactly had happened between Percy and her cousin; whether he had indeed hit Robert for no good reason. Whether Percy intended to continue seeing his mistress, and if so how often; and what did she look like, and how long it had been going on, and didn't he think he should have admitted to her that he had a mistress of long standing — most especially because she'd given him the opportunity so to do?

And didn't he think, then, that she, his wife, would ever be able to satisfy him, to please him, when the last time it had been so . . . so special?

Usually at this point Patricia found that she'd stopped pacing and was trying hard to fight back tears. *This won't do,* she told herself. She'd never been a simpering miss; she'd always been sensible and realistic.

How come, then, that where Percy was concerned she had suddenly become anything but sensible, her every instinct telling her to hurl herself at him the moment he appeared, melting as his strong arms came round her and giving herself up to the moment?

And then, suddenly, the moment was upon her. She heard the rattle of the carriage drawing up outside and thought for a moment she might swoon from the excitement.

Should she hurry into the large imposing hall to greet him, or stay here in the small secluded morning room? Would he come to find her, seek her out? Had he missed her as much as she'd missed him? Did he feel totally sick with anticipation as did she?

One thing was for sure, he couldn't possibly feel as confused.

It would take him a few minutes to remove his hat, to maybe have a few words with staff. She was foolish to have such a beating heart; after all, it was only Percy, the husband of an arranged marriage. It would be best if she were cool, standing perhaps like so, before the long windows, calmly contemplating nature.

The door burst open. Percy looked as

he had the first time she'd met him, flushed and slightly dishevelled, his warm brown eyes burning in his face. She met his fiery gaze, her heart thumping uncomfortably in her breast. She took two steps towards him.

'Oh, Percy,' said Lady Pat.

'Oh, Lady Pat,' said Lord Alexander, crushing her to him as though there was no tomorrow.

'I'm so glad you're home.'

'So am I,' said Percy punctuating his words with kisses. 'Missed you so much, Pat . . . I haven't got a mistress in York, I promise you. Should have made myself clear. I don't need a mistress. I've got you. You're all I need. Everything I need . . . Who'd have thought it? Never believed in love before.'

'Neither did I,' murmured Patricia, nestling happily against his shoulder.

Percy held her away from him for a moment.

'Does that mean — that you love me?'

Patricia nodded. 'When you almost

knocked me off my feet, Percy, I think I fell in love with you then, before I ever knew who you were.'

Incredulously, he looked at her. 'Lordy, Lady Pat, it was the same for me. Just couldn't believe what my heart was telling me. When I found out you were Mrs Pickering I felt — ' He searched around for the word. 'Desolate, quite desolate beyond belief . . . Then when I met you again and found out you were a widow, it just seemed so right. And it was so right! Is so right . . . Isn't it?' he asked anxiously, his left eyebrow lifting.

For an answer Patricia kissed him again before drawing him to sit next to her on the sofa.

'There are some things we must talk about. Things that I don't quite understand . . . I met Robert.'

A cloud passed over Percy's expression.

'It was quite by chance. I expected him to at least apologise for not attending my wedding.'

'And did he?'

183

'No. He seemed to think you'd told me about some kind of . . . 'falling-out' he called it, between you?'

'Ah, that,' said Percy. 'Yes, I'm very much afraid I found myself obliged to plant your cousin a facer.'

'A facer? You mean you knocked him down?'

'Fraid so,' admitted Percy cheerfully.

'But why?'

'He's pretty astute, your cousin. More brains than I credited him with. It occurred to him that even though you'd arranged matters so that he would benefit from your death after your marriage to me, he would stand to gain even more if your demise came before your marriage.'

'Good God!' Patricia's eyes widened in disbelief.

'Good God indeed,' repeated Percy, smiling grimly. 'I found a piece of hawthorn tucked under your horse's saddle. I returned it to him . . . He won't trouble us again.'

So it was true. Percy had done

something she'd wanted to do all her life — he'd knocked her cousin down. Patricia smiled. How very satisfying to know.

'I wish I'd seen you knock him down . . . And to think that not too long ago he wanted nothing better than to marry me!'

Percy tightened his grip around her shoulders. 'Thank God you said no.'

'Yes, thank God,' echoed Patricia.

She looked up at him hesitantly. 'I'm sorry I was so silly before you left. I'd gone downstairs, you see, and overheard some stupid talk about your having a mistress in York.'

'Did have,' corrected Percy. 'It finished when my father died. Glad to say she's someone else's mistress now. Told you before — don't want a mistress now I'm a married man. Have to be out of my senses to want one when I'm married to you.'

Patricia felt her face grow hot. 'Percy, the last time — you know! It was — did you think . . . I mean, I wasn't the only one who found it to be — well . . . very, very special?'

'Very special indeed,' answered Percy softly. 'We'll do it again. In fact, we'll make every time special.' His eyes grew dark as he looked at her. 'In fact, half a mind to start now. That family we want to have? No time like the present, eh? Tell the servants — don't want to be disturbed.'

Patricia gave a low chuckle. 'Just one thing . . . '

Percy drew away slightly. 'What's that, my love?'

With shining eyes, Patricia smoothed her hands over the curve of her stomach. 'I think we might have succeeded already.'

She watched anxiously as a look of incredulity was followed by a smile of delight that washed over her husband's features.

'Calls for a celebration, Lady Pat. Tell me, how should we celebrate? A little lie down in our room, perhaps?'

Patricia chuckled again.

'I love the way you laugh, Lady Pat.'

'I love the way you call me 'Lady Pat'.'
'I love that you are Lady Pat.'
'I love your eyebrow — the left one.'
'What's wrong with the right one?'
'Nothing. Absolutely nothing,' said Lady Pat, reaching up to kiss it.

THE END

We do hope that you have enjoyed reading this large print book.

Did you know that all of our titles are available for purchase?

We publish a wide range of high quality large print books including:
Romances, Mysteries, Classics
General Fiction
Non Fiction and Westerns

Special interest titles available in large print are:
The Little Oxford Dictionary
Music Book, Song Book
Hymn Book, Service Book

Also available from us courtesy of Oxford University Press:
Young Readers' Dictionary
(large print edition)
Young Readers' Thesaurus
(large print edition)

For further information or a free brochure, please contact us at:
Ulverscroft Large Print Books Ltd.,
The Green, Bradgate Road, Anstey,
Leicester, LE7 7FU, England.
Tel: (00 44) 0116 236 4325
Fax: (00 44) 0116 234 0205

SHADOWS OF DANGER

Angela Dracup

Diana is uneasy when she has a premonition of an air disaster. But when she meets charismatic widower Louis, she is terrified — for he is the man in her dream. Soon she is in love with Louis, but her fear for his safety becomes acute. It seems the only way she can protect him is to marry a man she does not love. Would Louis ever forgive her for leaving him? Would true love eventually win through?

TO LOVE AGAIN

Chrissie Loveday

It is 1945 and the lives of families have changed. The pain and memories of the war years have left their mark. Lizzie Vale, the carefree girl — once an aspiring journalist — has changed and become a dedicated nurse. She fights to help her patients recover from their terrible injuries and falls in love with Daniel Miles. Could they ever have a future? Injuries and family prejudice present seemingly insuperable obstacles, but Lizzie is a force to be reckoned with.

HEARTS AND CRAFTS

Wendy Kremer

Eduardo Noriega struggles financially with running the family estate in Spain. He's also responsible for the farm, his mother and Maria, a family servant. When some furniture is in need of urgent renovation friends recommend Claire, who travels to Casona de la Esquina from England — despite the expense involved. Her arrival upsets Elena, a neighbour's daughter, who imagined waltzing down the aisle with Eduardo. Claire does her job, uncovers an intriguing family secret . . . and changes everyone's plans, including her own.

LAST MINUTE ROMANCE

Sheila Holroyd

Etta Sanderson has to fly to Turkey unexpectedly to help Kaan Talbot guide a group of tourists around the country. At first Kaan resents her inexperience, but they begin to appreciate each other's abilities. When they discover that some of the tourists are using the trip as a cover for criminal activities, Kaan and Etta work together to frustrate their schemes — but despite this success, is it too soon to think of planning a future together?

LIGHT OF MY LIFE

Janet Whitehead

1840s Cornwall. Meg Deveral and her father, victims of a great injustice, were powerless to right the wrong committed against them. When Jack Masterman arrived in the fishing village of Penderow, he vowed to get justice for the Deverals. But the guilty parties were ruthless in protecting their interests. Meg and Jack faced murder, abduction and a desperate race against time before they could finally admit that, in each other, they'd found the one true light of their life.

POLKA DOT DREAMS

Julia Douglas

Natty loves vintage clothes and fabulous fifties music, so she thinks she's found her perfect man when she meets Matt, who runs a rock 'n' roll themed ice-cream parlour. However, Matt's life is rather complicated — will Cameron, the mysterious Scottish Teddy Boy promising to make her a singing star, turn Natty's head? Natty finds an ally in Matt's mum, Margie, a seaside landlady, but can she really find an old-fashioned love in this rock 'n' roll romance?